EMB

EMBER

Book 7
The Happily Never After Series

By

HP Mallory

10 Chosen Ones:
When a pall is cast upon the land,
Despair not, mortals,
For come forth heroes ten.
One in oceans deep,
One the flame shall keep,
One a fae,
One a cheat,
One shall poison grow,
One for death,
One for chaos,
One for control,
One shall pay a magic toll.

CHAPTER ONE
EMBER

It's been a long day, and I'm looking forward to climbing into bed.

The drudgery in this office is endless, but it suits me, because I have complete order here and 'order' should be my middle name. I rarely have any need to leave this place and while that might sound antisocial and lonely, I prefer it that way.

I used to have a home outside this cold government building, but the events that happened there keep me from returning. My sister, Marzella, still lives in the unkempt hovel with our mother. Personally, I can't fathom stepping foot in the place after what happened to our younger sister, Talia.

Neither my mother nor my sisters have ever been particularly kind to me, but they're the only family I have and I do love them. Now, as I remember the events of that day, I still shudder as I recall the piles of junk falling down on us—evidence of years and years of my mother's hoarding. I struggled to breathe beneath layers of old parchments and secondhand books— books that were never even read. Buried as I was, no one attempted to come to my rescue, so I had to tunnel my own way out. Still, I persevered and eventually escaped.

1

As soon as I emerged from the rubble, I found Talia, her outstretched arm just a little distance from me. Forgetting my own trauma for the moment, I started to dig her out. Although I did my best, it was ultimately hopeless. Talia had been standing near a shelf that toppled on her, crushing her under its merciless weight. I'll never forget her unfocused eyes, or the indentation scored into her forehead by a jagged crystal perched atop the mess. It was the ultimate irony too: the same stone that killed her contained symbols intended to ward off death.

One would think I'd be fairly ambivalent about the death of a girl who'd been so horrid to me, but I was still devastated. Despite all her faults, Talia was my family. Truly, her death was quite traumatic since I was the one blamed, even though it was in no way my fault.

Shaking off the bad memory, I begin to rise from my desk in order to leave my office for the evening.

A stranger's voice coming from the other room draws my attention toward the entryway. He's just asked for me and, curious, I step toward the slightly open door, wondering why he's come.

Watching him, I note how he waves one hand as he speaks, revealing deep scars across his skin. I wonder what might have caused them. But, his scars aren't his most interesting characteristic. That would be his eyes. They're deep and telling and with his hand gestures, he seems as if he'd be suited to the stage. The more I study him, the more I find I don't want to pull my gaze away and that's a dangerous sign—in my experience, it's better to avoid all emotional connections with people because they only end up in pain, especially where men are concerned.

I chuckle inwardly as the tiny imp receptionist, Cecilia, informs him I'm not here. She tells everyone the same, hoping they'll go away rather than bother me. She's good at acting the part of gate-keeper given her overall disposition, which isn't exactly "friendly" in nature.

When the man sighs with exasperation, something about his reaction inspires me to be bolder than normal and I step out of the shadows, without even realizing what I'm doing.

"You're looking for me?" I ask.

"Are you Ember Limus?" the man replies as he turns to face me.

Despite the sandy brown hair falling in shaggy layers around his face, I can see his pale blue eyes brightening as they settle on me. He's handsome—more so than I originally thought and surprise ricochets through me, much though I try to ignore it. Well, more like surprise and something that feels like humming in my gut.

I answer his question with a simple "I am."

In the meantime, I pause for a moment to further take in his appearance. He's dressed in fine clothes that, based on their tailored cut and silken fabric, are indicative of the Anoka Desert. The extra coat makes me assume he's not used to the cold in our part of the world.

The stranger offers no response to my reply. Instead, he just stands there, gawking at me like a fool.

While it's not an uncommon reaction from men, I've little use for such nonsense. Physical beauty matters very little to me, even though it seems to be first in importance for everyone else.

Instead, I grow impatient as I watch others leaving for the day and I want to do the same. At least, what passes for "leaving for the day" in my case—it's not as though I go very far, considering my sleeping quarters are in the basement of this building.

I give the stranger another moment to gather his wits before prodding him. "Have you come only to stare at me?" I ask, a bit bemused when he suddenly clears his throat and colors a bit in his cheeks. There's certainly a part of me that's quite dumbfounded at my own bold comment. Usually, I choose not to make conversation with anyone and certainly not to taunt them. And yet, there's something about this man that makes me want to taunt him—something that makes me want him to admit he finds me attractive.

Ember, what in the blazes has gotten into you? I ask myself, but I have no answer.

"I, uh, no, of course not." He awkwardly pulls himself up to his full height and he easily towers over me by at least a head.

"Oh?" I ask with a little laugh.

He nods insistently. "I'm Aimes Padmoore. I've been told you're the best cartographer in the land."

"That would be accurate." There's no pride in my words. It's merely a correct assessment of my abilities in this field.

Mr. Padmoore extends a rolled-up scroll that I just

now notice was under his arm the whole time. Really, I should have been paying less attention to those fathomless blue eyes. "I need your help with a map given to me by the Blue Faerie."

His mention of the Blue Faerie catches me off guard, making me hesitate. What could he possibly need from me and, furthermore, how in the world has he acquired a map from the Blue Faerie? My gaze falls from his handsome face to the proffered scroll and my curiosity overrules the exhaustion I felt just moments ago. Waving my arm in the direction of my office, I invite him in, saying, "Well, then... let's have a look, shall we?"

My boldness quickly dissipates as he approaches. I'm unaccustomed to men standing in such close proximity, nevermind within my personal workspace. And now it's just the two of us... alone and in my office. I swallow hard as I further ponder it.

As to Aimes Padmoore's physical characteristics—he's *very* attractive. More so than I'd previously imagined. And there's something rugged about him. He's obviously wealthy, given his state of dress, but there's something beneath the refined clothing and genteel manners. Something that speaks to the feral man inside. Perhaps it's his eyes?

Or perhaps you ate something bad for dinner that's assaulting your senses, I think to myself.

Regardless, Mr. Padmoore appears to be quite genteel and charming. He has a soft but kind smile which immediately puts me on edge because men are only nice when they want something and that something is usually nestled between a woman's thighs. For that reason alone, I dress very conservatively and keep my distance from any and all men. Some might call me *frigid*, but the truth is, I just don't trust men's intentions. And this one is no different.

The way Mr. Padmoore looks at me confirms my initial assessment, however, he surprises me by stopping short of my door. Glancing down at the scroll, he lets out a loud sigh before looking up at me again.

"Now that I've bothered to pay attention to my surroundings—I realize it's late and your fellow associates have all gone home for the night."

"Yes," I reply, not sure what he's driving at.

"Could I bother you for a few more minutes of your time?"

That would require the two of us—alone—in my office. Something I'm definitely not comfortable with. "I… the work day is over and I have… I have a busy evening ahead of me." Lies, of course, but he doesn't need to know that.

"Two more minutes, I promise," he says. "I will lay the scroll out on your table and you can tell me what you think, and I'll be on my way."

"I… I'm not comfortable being… alone with a stranger in my office," I admit finally.

He clears his throat again, the awkwardness once more rising to the fore. "Perhaps we could reschedule this meeting?" He flicks his eyes around the increasingly unpopulated building.

"Yes," I reply, a little too quickly because I'm suddenly aware of the fact that Cecilia is packing up to leave and that will mean I'll be alone with Mr. Padmoore. Very alone with him…

I've never been alone with a man before and I don't want to start now. I swallow hard as I think about it and beads of sweat start along my brow.

"Then shall we agree to meet tomorrow?" he suggests.

"T… tomorrow is my day… my day off," I answer, cursing myself for the hesitation in my voice. I'm nervous and I'm sure Mr. Padmoore can ascertain as much.

"I understand it's your day off and I hate to bother you with this request, but it's incredibly… urgent. If I make it worth your while, could we meet in the rock garden at noon tomorrow?"

"I don't… know if that's a good idea," I reply, nervously scratching my arm. Truthfully, my head is already spinning at the thought of seeing this man again and leaving the confines of the safety of my office. And to work on an unscheduled day, no less!

Under his coat, he fishes out a pouch from his belt before handing it to me. "I will happily pay you for your time. Will this suffice?"

Accepting it, I undo the strings of the pouch and stare at the contents for a moment. There's a lot of money inside, much more than I'd expect for the task of deciphering a map—even if on my day off. And the truth is: I need the money. My income barely sustains me, let alone my mother and sister. And business has been slow lately. In fact, I'm almost out of money, thanks to family matters beyond my control.

I cinch up the purse strings and nod. "Okay."

You're agreeing to be alone with this… this man, Ember! I remind myself. *What if he… what if he decides to overpower you and force you into the bushes somewhere? And then what unmentionable things will he do to you?*

He could do those same unmentionable things to me here and now, I argue in response as I realize Cecilia has already left.

Mr. Padmoore gives me a relieved half-smile. "Very good, Ms. Limus. Until then."

I watch him turn and make his way out the front doors as my heart pounds against my ribs in outrage over the fact that I might very well have set myself up for something… unpleasant. Once Padmoore leaves, I cross the lobby to lock the doors. Afterwards, I return to the safety of my office and start putting things in order for the night as I try to talk my heart into beating normally.

My workday finally over, I exit through the door at the back of the office. On the other side, I descend the stairs to the basement quarters I inhabit. All the while, I wonder how I can talk myself out of meeting Padmoore tomorrow.

You took his money… there's no way to back out now.

My accommodations are walled off from the rest of the basement and can only be entered from my office above or from another door on the back bedroom wall. The second door leads to another set of stairs that terminate in a small concrete patio on the side of the building. I keep that door secured with a large tumble lock and a sturdy vanity resting against it, but even with all my safety precautions, I still feel… vulnerable.

And I'm sure these feelings of… fear have everything to do with the sudden visit from this stranger.

Despite my valiant attempts at sleep, it eludes me.

My mind keeps spinning with questions. What does this Aimes Padmoore possibly need to decipher regarding the map? And how is the Blue Faerie involved? Then I consider the prospect of meeting with him—of seeing him again—of being *alone* with him.

I pull out the aforementioned pouch from underneath my pillow and study it. Pouring the coins onto my bedside table, I realize I underestimated the amount of money inside. There are even more coins than I originally thought—easily more than I make in one week.

It's just simply one meeting in a public place! I tell myself. *You'll inform Mr. Padmoore about the map, then you both will be on your way and you'll never have to see him again.*

But, I don't want to go! I really, really don't want to go…

Regardless, I gave the man my word, and that means I'll have to meet him. Gathering the coins, I return them to the pouch, and push the bedside table out to reveal a small vent in the wall. I move the vent cover aside and place the coins within. Then I replace the cover before moving the table back into place.

My quarters are always spotless.

A lifetime of compulsive disorders lends itself to keeping my abode in good order. And order doesn't just apply to my living quarters, whether I'm creating a map or just making sure every surface around me gleams. I'm meticulous in everything I do. I'm also extra careful not to scrape the floor each time I move the table, because doing so would leave telltale marks revealing my hiding spot to anyone who cares to look. Not that anyone would, but it's my belief that it's better to be safe than sorry.

I lie down on the bed again, closing my eyes, straining to sleep. Instead, my imagination drifts to those rough, scarred hands of Mr. Padmoore and I wonder how they might feel on my skin. At the thought, I start to sweat and my nipples harden into pebbles. Despite my wariness of men, my libido knows no such fear and welcomes the opposite sex. It's a constant battle between the heathen within and the proper lady without. And at this moment, the heathen is victorious—cajoling me into removing my nightgown as I touch the intimate center of my being.

I moan and quickly bring myself to orgasm in a carefully choreographed, practiced fashion. There's no danger of being heard, not here in the depths of this old building. It's only patrolled from the outside after hours, safeguarding the precious documents inside.

The climax provides the relaxation I need, and its calming effect settles my nerves. Finally, I'm able to drift into a mostly peaceful sleep. Still, all the questions regarding Aimes Padmoore remain before I finally fade into the gray mists of unconsciousness.

CHAPTER TWO
EMBER

My deep sleep ends rather abruptly.

The clock on my wall, its face illuminated by a faerie dust compound, shows the time: 4:30 AM. Dawn is still a good three hours away. I rise with a groan, knowing why I'm restless. The meeting with Aimes Padmoore still disturbs me. I find myself torn at the prospect of leaving a place where I'm fully protected in exchange for the allure of the map and the man bearing it.

Don't be silly, Ember, I tell myself. *You're only interested in the Blue Faerie's map, not in Aimes Padmoore.*

But, the more I argue that fact with myself, the more I realize I'm arguing it in the first place. I try to calm myself by polishing the brass rails of my bed, then replacing the bed linens with freshly laundered ones. I drop the dirty linens into a hamper, then wash them with a bucket and washboard I salvaged from my family's home. The building has a laundry service, of course, but they fail to meet my cleanliness standards. Besides, I prefer to clean my own things.

After I finish my chores, I dress for the day. A pair of candles on either side of the vanity mirror gives me a full-length view of my appearance, and I fuss with the collar of my blouse for far too long. Honestly, I don't know why I chose this top. It's nearly impossible to keep the large bow at the neck straight. Finally, I admit defeat and swap it for a high-collared, white, button-up blouse instead. Indeed, it's the perfect match for the tawny slacks I've already picked out. Yes, so much better.

Climbing the stairs to my office, I fret with every step. My anxiety doesn't decrease one iota as I go about my morning tasks. Usually, my head is clear and I feel ready to face the day after my morning routine. But now all I can think about is the map waiting for me in the garden. Not to mention, the mysterious man from the desert who bears it.

I return to my desk and decide to busy myself with my work while I wait for the proper time to depart… in order to meet Mr. Padmoore. Shortly after dawn finally breaks, my tattered nerves return to their frayed state.

For hours, I continuously glance at the clock, ready to jump out of my skin before it's time to meet the handsome stranger. To distract myself, I focus on what I know about him thus far. First, the clothing he wore; could he not be royalty? Or perhaps a nobleman? But I dismiss that notion once I further ponder it. Men of such lofty status are rarely given to timid behavior such that I witnessed yesterday—timid as in: refusing to meet my eyes, clearing his throat repeatedly and, at one point, even blushing. Yet it's obvious Mr. Padmoore has plenty of money, owing to the expensive fabrics of his clothing. I find myself wanting to know more about him… even craving that knowledge. Truly, I don't know what's gotten into me, but I don't like it. Ordinarily, I am indifferent to men—even handsome ones. And yet this man… no matter how hard I attempt it, I can't seem to keep him out of my mind.

Eventually, my eyes land on the clock again, and I watch the long minutes crawl by as noon gradually approaches. When 11:40 clicks into place, I steel myself and stand, smoothing down my blouse and slacks before stepping out of my office, as it will take a good twenty minutes to reach the rock garden.

I begin walking past the receptionist desk toward the front doors. Each step takes every ounce of willpower I possess, slowly propelling me forward. My elevated heels make loud clicking sounds on the marble floor, in time with the beating of my heart.

I know Cecilia is watching me, but I choose not to acknowledge her. Unfortunately, she doesn't give me the same courtesy.

"What are you doing?" she inquires, her small voice taking on a metallic quality. That's owing to the bullhorn on her desk that amplifies her vocalizations.

I'm grateful to have to stop and turn around to face her because it buys me more time. "I'm going… out."

She raises a nearly invisible eyebrow in astonishment and repeats, "*You're* going out?"

"Yes," I say impatiently, stretching out the single syllable as though it were a rubber band.

She gives a small grunt. Not disapproval exactly, but certainly surprise. "And when will you return?"

"I don't know," I admit truthfully. "Hopefully, not too long."

But hopefully long enough to find out more about Mr. Padmoore, I think, before I can stop myself.

Cecilia is silent as she considers my reply. Though she eventually grunts once more, she doesn't speak again, but returns to whatever was occupying her on her desk as though my whereabouts are an interesting but minor detail to her day. I suppose they are.

The conversation clearly over, I turn around and walk through the doors. The second I do, I immediately want to turn back. The sunlight is too bright, far brighter than the rays that steal through the windows in my office. I sense an all-pervading doom hanging over me, poised to strike at any moment.

"Just focus on the task at hand, Ember," I say, forcing myself to continue walking. "Focus... it's just a job... a *well-paying* job and one you need... one *your family* needs." I chant similar platitudes the entire walk to the rock garden. If anyone notices my self-absorbed conversation, they give no sign.

Approximately eighteen minutes later—thank you, Talia, for the posthumously endowed pocket watch—I arrive at the rock garden. Although my heart is still racing, I have time to spare. That soothes my nerves somewhat.

As the garden is quite deserted this time of day, I quickly stride the path that leads to the center. I soon spot Mr. Padmoore, who stands next to the improbable beanstalk fountain, the garden's centerpiece.

Oh, no, I realize with some horror, *he's not alone!*

The other man does his best to keep a low profile, his head and face obscured by a brown hood attached to a cloak. He pretends to casually look over the beanstalk while ignoring Mr. Padmoore. But I don't fail to notice he only speaks when Mr. Padmoore isn't doing likewise; and that's the giveaway. Even donning the cloak, this man's stature and poise is much more confident than that of my new employer, suggesting he might be Mr. Padmoore's superior. He stands at about equal height to Mr. Padmoore—I would guess them both to be six feet.

I fight the urge to turn and flee all the way back to the office. But, Mr. Padmoore is a client and I've already made it this far. Not to mention the fact that I still want to see and study the Blue Faerie's map. And I also must admit I'm curious regarding both men before me. Who is the man in the cloak, what relation is he to Mr. Padmoore and what do they want with the Blue Faerie's map?

The other man looks up as he hears me approaching before quickly looking away. But, too late. Even with the disguise of his hood, I recognize him easily. After all, I've memorized every detail of his face whenever I see his portrait in the Hall of Records. To his credit, he gives up any pretense of being a bystander as I approach. I can feel a flush spreading on my cheeks when he steps up beside Mr. Padmoore to greet me.

For his part, Mr. Padmoore checks his pocket watch and smiles. "Right on time, Ms. Limus."

"As promised," I reply, channeling as much customary professionalism into my voice as possible, yet I can't take my eyes off his hooded companion. I'm just in… complete shock. How is it possible that standing before me is the Prince of Sweetland? Thinking I might do better to act taken in by his guise, I don't allow my surprise to show and I play as if I don't recognize him. "I don't recall you mentioning another party would be present for this discussion."

The would-be stranger smiles under his hood. "I was under the impression you wouldn't want to be overly *crowded* in your office. Besides, I was a bit tied up with other details last night and could not accompany Aimes."

"I see," I reply, feeling a bit embarrassed, because it's apparent Mr. Padmoore discussed my behavior earlier when I let it be known I wasn't comfortable with just the two of us in my office. What must they think of me? That I'm a silly weakling and afraid of men? I suppose it's not far from the truth.

Mr. Padmoore merely replies, "Ember Limus, meet Prince Blakely Nonpareil."

Now that Mr. Padmoore has introduced him and his identity is no longer secret, I figure I can drop my own ruse. "Yes, I'm very much aware of His Highness's true identity," I say, while I extend my hand politely. Even as my heartbeat increases at the prospect of touching the prince's hand, I reproach myself because I'm far too dignified to act like a common school girl with a crush.

And yet, the prince is handsome. Just as handsome as Mr. Padmoore but in a different way. Where Mr. Padmoore is fairly light in his features—lightish hair and skin and blue eyes—the prince has dark brown hair, darker eyes and an olive complexion. When he smiles, he has one dimple in his left cheek and his eyes sparkle with mischief. Rumors around Sweetland are that he's very popular with the ladies and standing before him now, I can understand why.

His Highness leans down to kiss my hand as he all but purrs, "It's a pleasure to meet you, Ms. Limus."

This marks the first time I manage to resist the urge to reach for my handkerchief to wipe away his germs. Yes, I'm quite fussy and fastidious about cleanliness and ensuring all things around me and upon me are in order. Germs certainly aren't in order.

Focusing on the prince's handsome face, I can see beyond his hood and I can firmly say the Hall of Records' portrait doesn't do the prince's fine features justice.

Bringing my mind back to the matter at hand, I ask, "Would I be overstepping my bounds, Your Highness, if I asked why you are here?"

"Not at all," the prince replies with a ready smile that I'm quite sure has melted the heart of many a maid. Good thing for me I'm not taken in by such uselessly gallant overtures. He makes a show of looking around. "Perhaps we could sit by the fountain to discuss?"

"As you please, Your Highness."

"Please," he says, holding up his hand, "call me Blake. I'm not one for pomp and circumstance."

I want to laugh at that, given the fact that 'pomp and circumstance' is his birthright, but I say nothing.

"It appears, from what I've thus far gathered, that Ms. Limus happens to disagree with such informality," Mr. Padmoore opines.

His Highness—*Blake*—all but rolls his eyes. "There's respect and then there's obsequiousness, Aimes. I really need to teach you the difference sometime." Then he seems to remember my presence and says, "But that is another matter for another day." He gestures towards the nearest bench. "Shall we?"

I'm not keen to sit on any of the filthy benches, of course, but the prince—*Blake*—is so charming, I can't refuse. So, I walk with them, pleased when Blake takes the time to dust off one of the benches with his own handkerchief. Once he finishes, he, Mr. Padmoore, and I take our seats. While the bench isn't exactly clean, it's certainly an improvement.

I watch Mr. Padmoore pull out the familiar piece of parchment from inside his coat and he hands it to me. I unfold it carefully and immediately take note of the odd markings and notations. It's obviously a puzzle of some sort. I turn the parchment from side to side, trying to determine the proper angle to view it.

Of course, studying the map makes a welcome distraction from the two incredibly handsome men sitting on either side of me, both of whom are staring at me with unconcealed interest.

Of course they are, Ember, because they want to know what you make of the map!

I can't help the sense of disappointment that flows through me.

"Now that you've seen it," Blake says, "I'm sure you can understand why we need your help."

"It's my understanding," Mr. Padmoore continues, "that you're the best at decoding such ciphers, Ms. Limus. Indeed, it's popular knowledge that you've surpassed some of the best minds in His Highness's—"

The prince raises an eyebrow, which causes Mr. Padmoore to retract and say, "Sorry, *Blake's* kingdom, with your superior deduction skills."

To be told such sweet compliments by so handsome a man stirs up all kinds of things inside me. Things that used to be basically nonexistent—things I'd firmly stuck a lid on whenever they happened to surface. Suddenly, I find myself desperate to escape this situation and both handsome strangers. As the seconds tick by, I earnestly search for a way out.

There is no way out when Mr. Padmoore has already paid you, I remind myself.

I can and will happily return their investment, just as long as I never have to see either one of them ever again.

Yes, this… these feelings… this overwhelming attraction I feel towards both of them—it's too much for me to handle. This entire morning has been too much for me to handle.

I inhale deeply and then shake my head. "I'm afraid your informants are exaggerating. I'm just a glorified librarian, nothing more." Of course, my comment is pure bunk, but I'm hopeful they won't see the lie.

"I refuse to believe that for a single moment," Blake counters, shaking his head. "All reports from Aimes—whose information I absolutely trust—are consistent. You have an exceptional mind, and that is exactly what we desperately need right now."

Praise from not just one fine specimen of manhood, but two? I clear my throat and look up from the parchment as I realize escape isn't going to be easily achieved—not when it's fairly obvious these two are determined in their enterprise. I breathe in deeply again and try to calm my frantic heart.

Just review the map, tell them what they want to know, and they'll be on their merry way and you'll never have to see them again and you can go right back to your boring and beyond sheltered life.

"Very well. In light of your faith in my abilities as well as your generous payment, I shall see what I can do."

Blake smiles at me. "I could ask for no less."

I hold up the object of my inquiry and then shake my head. "This isn't something that I can give you an answer about immediately," I say, as I wonder if such was what they were expecting. "I need time to study the map in order to unlock its complexities."

"We understand," Blake says. "And there are plenty of bright and quiet spaces within the palace where you could accomplish such study."

At the thought of attending the palace, I feel my heart start to beat in earnest and I wish the ground would open up and swallow me whole. I clear my throat and then face Blake's smiling and welcoming expression with one a little less welcoming. "May I take the map with me instead?" Blake appears hesitant and I realize I need to further explain. "I always work better at my desk… in solitude."

Mr. Padmoore and Blake share a look between them. "I think I speak for both of us," Mr. Padmoore replies, "when I say the *how* is less important than the actual results."

"With that said," Blake adds, "what can you tell us at this moment?"

I turn my attention back to the scroll and allow my brain to begin its magic. It's always been a gift, this unique concentration of mine—when I study something, it's almost as if I can see it in a three-dimensional way. As if the maps become more than a flat piece of parchment. As if the landscape begins to grow before my eyes, revealing its peaks and valleys, its towns and forests.

My unparalleled abilities aside, this cipher is quite baffling. Rather like quicksilver, certain fragments trigger my brain only to slip between my metaphorical fingers. After what feels like a long time—but is actually only five minutes, per Mr. Padmoore's open watch—everything clicks into place. I don't need to take the map back to my desk after all!

I smile broadly as I glance over at the prince. "You are correct about it being a map... Blake," I say, catching myself before using his noble title.

Blake purses his kissable lips (and how or why I even notice they are kissable is beyond me) and nods. "Agreed, but what sort of map is it?"

"It refers to a certain location in the next principality," I reply, tapping my finger on the relevant spot. "That would be Ascor, unless I'm mistaken. There, you'll find another map that will also need deciphering."

Mr. Padmoore looks at me in fascination. "What makes you so certain?"

I shrug. "Simple logic... if this map is protected by symbols, it naturally follows that the next map will be likewise. Whatever the ultimate destination the Blue Faerie is pointing you towards, it's meant for you alone to know."

"And where precisely in Ascor is our next map?" Blake wonders aloud.

I look at the map again, searching for the answer and find it momentarily. "It's buried beneath a lyre."

"A lyre?" he repeats, his brows pinching together in a vexed expression. "Are you sure?"

"Positive," I respond, then realize I need to amend my statement. "However, I think it likely not to be an *actual* lyre, but rather a tavern."

"Why?" Mr. Padmoore asks, leaning forward.

"Part of my duties is filing and classifying tax receipts," I explain. "I recall a recent receipt referencing a now closed tavern in Ascor called The Wicked Lyre."

Mr. Padmoore looks at Blake with a raised eyebrow. "Rather an interesting coincidence this next map would be *there* of all places, yes?"

Blake hums and looks at me. "And are you quite certain we'll find the next map at The Wicked Lyre?"

"I'm certain," I reply, reaching into my pants pocket. I pull out a capped inkpot and a fine quill. "May I?" I ask as I point the quill to the map. Blake nods. Uncapping the pot, I dip my quill and quickly make notations on the map that swiftly turn it into something a layperson could understand. I'm certain to include a compass in my notations so they know exactly where to go.

Then I roll up the scroll and hand it back to Mr. Padmoore. "These notes will take you where you wish to go," I tell him before I retrieve and store away my inkpot and quill.

Mr. Padmoore looks the map over before handing it to Blake, whose eyes sparkle with fascination as he smiles first at me, then at his associate.

"As ever, Aimes," he says, his focus securely fastened on the parchment. "Your judgment remains impeccable." I figure he's referring to me and my abilities.

Mr. Padmoore allows himself a smile while Blake puts the map down. "On the basis of this exceptional work," he says as he looks back at me, "I must request more of your services."

More work? That means seeing them both again? I immediately feel panic begin welling up within me. This visit was one of the most difficult things I've accomplished in months. I can't imagine having a second one. "I don't…" I start, but Blake interrupts.

"Naturally, the pay will increase since you've just proven yourself imperative to our cause," he says, adopting the same tone I gave him when he asked whether I had correctly deciphered the map. "For services such as yours, money is irrelevant."

"Oh, well," I say, rising from the bench as I search for any excuse not to see them again. "I am quite busy, you know."

"Name your price, Ember Limus," Blake says. "Whatever fee you want."

"Well," I start and then promptly lose my voice—mainly because the way he just said my name—it's too intimate for words. It's as if he said my name after removing himself from inside me. As if he knows me in intimate ways, no man has ever known me.

Think, Ember, think of an excuse! I rail at myself, but my brain is suddenly empty. "After you retrieve this next map, you can—"

"Actually," Mr. Padmoore interrupts, after clearing his throat. "We actually… need you to come with us."

I look between both men in confusion, but both just smile back at me. Soon my confusion turns to shock when I realize just what they're asking of me and then that shock turns to horror. "Come with you?" I repeat, shaking my head, as if I can't understand his words. Panic begins to bubble up again. "Oh, I couldn't… I couldn't possibly come with you! I… well, I have work to do! I have clients and… and responsibilities!"

Mr. Padmoore shakes his head. "I'm quite certain your company can spare you while you are in the service of the prince."

"Particularly after I dispatch a representative to explain as much, minus *certain* details, of course," Blake adds.

"I," I start and promptly swallow my tongue.

"Ms. Limus, this errand is of the utmost importance," Mr. Padmoore says.

"I appreciate your faith in me and my abilities, Mr. Padmoore," I start.

"Please, call me Aimes."

I swallow even harder. I can't... I can't call him Aimes! It's bad enough I'm already calling the prince by his first name. Oh, this entire business is way too close for comfort. "I simply... can't travel with you... both." I gasp, backing away from them. Don't they understand? Can't they see how difficult it was for me to come here—to this silly garden? What makes them think I'm capable of crossing whole kingdoms and traveling with the two of them? Without a chaperone? It's indecent!

"Please, Ember," Mr. Padmoore, er Aimes, nearly begs. "No one else can understand maps the way you can. And we can ill-afford to waste more time trying to find someone."

"Someone who doesn't exist," Blake adds.

I stare at the looming beanstalk fountain. The great giant appears ready to crush me at a blow. And I suddenly wish he would—just so I canavoid this situation. I look at them and their expressions are yearning but also hard. They won't take no for an answer.

"I… I simply can't!" I babble, my long-suppressed panic clearly emerging as I turn to start walking back to my office. But as soon as I take a step, I find myself breaking into a full run.

"Ms. Limus!" Blake calls after me, but I'm already well on my way down the path. I no longer see the rock garden around me. Nor do I notice the cobblestones under my feet, nor the observant bystanders. All I can think about is hurrying back to the safety of my building—all I can think about is escaping the two of them and their hungry eyes.

I rush inside the front doors of my building and close them, trying desperately to catch my breath. After a few seconds, I lean against them as if I expect someone will try to force their way in.

"Ember?" Cecilia squeaks at me from her desk. "Are you all right?" Despite the tinny megaphone, I detect a note of worry in her voice.

"Yes, I'm fine," I lie, more ashamed of the truth than my fib. "I'm... just not feeling well."

"Shall I have someone fetch a doctor?"

In other circumstances, I might have laughed because such is Cecilia's standard solution for everything from a paper cut to a bad day at work.

"No, no, it's not serious," I insist, finally pushing myself away from the doors. Trying to ignore the creeping dread spiraling through me, I quickly cross the floor and pause at my office door.

"I need to lie down," I tell her. "If anyone asks for me, tell them I'm unavailable, please." I think about the insistence in Blake and Aimes's eyes. "In fact… tell anyone who asks that I'm not here."

Her thin lips break into a smirk. "Don't I always do a good job of keeping everyone away from you?"

I nod before rushing inside my office. Locking the door, I all but fly down the back stairs into my private quarters. I lock my door and then stripping off my clothes, I throw them into the hamper and climb into my bed. With a sigh, I pull the blankets over my head to hide from the horrible, demanding world outside. And more pointedly, the horrible and demanding expressions of two men who have somehow dug a tunnel into my brain. No matter how hard I fight it, I can't remove the memory of their eyes on me, their smiles…

CHAPTER THREE
BLAKE

Both Aimes and I stare at the path for several minutes after Ms. Limus's swift departure. "Well," I finally say to break the silence. "She certainly bolted like a scared rabbit."

"That she did, Your Highness," Aimes agrees with a sigh.

"*Blake*," I correct him (yet again).

"Apologies... you know how ingrained my habits are."

"Not as deep as this young woman's fears, apparently," I muse. "What can we do to get her to help us?"

"I wish I had a workable idea," Aimes admits on a shrug. "I have heard she is quite eccentric, but I suppose it's to be expected from someone of her particular genius."

"Eccentric, yes," I answer as I shake my head and draw to mind her light blond hair, green eyes and a body that has to be ripe beneath those marmish clothes. "You never warned me that she would be so... enticing."

Aimes swallows hard. "Blake, you must do your best to keep your libido within your trousers. Ember Limus is not the type of woman to seduce."

"Ah, come now, Aimes, where's the fun in that?"

He frowns at the ground beneath our feet. "Regardless, I was certain your presence would carry enough weight to commit her to our cause."

"And yet it seemed she was mostly… afraid of me," I answer, shaking my head because this Ember Limus is the strangest woman I've ever met. Beautiful, yes, but hers is the beauty of a porcelain doll—cold and fragile.

"Yes," Aimes responds.

I look over at him. "And strangely enough, she seemed scared of you, too."

"Perhaps she's afraid of men, in general?"

"What can we do then?" I ask in exasperation, throwing my hands into the air. "She's the only one who can solve those ciphers."

"Perhaps there is someone learned who could assist us," Aimes stammers. "But finding such an accomplished person would take time."

"And time is a luxury we don't have, my friend."

He nods ruefully. "I do have one idea for our predicament," Aimes says then.

"And what is that?"

He smiles. "We could seek a pint of ale and discuss it further while we wet our dry throats."

"That, my friend, sounds like a grand idea," I tell him on a chuckle. *And not just for the bittersweet taste this meeting left in my mouth*, I think to myself.

We both rise to our feet. "With your permission, I'll retrieve Vaughn while you find us a seat at the local pub."

I nod as we say our temporary goodbyes before parting through opposite ends of the rock garden.

Taking a seat at the back of the almost empty pub, I order all three of us a pint. Aimes has yet to return with Vaughn, but I can wait. Indeed, this brief moment of quiet gives me time to consider the enigmatic and lovely Ms. Ember Limus.

Physically, as I mentioned earlier, she is beautiful, stunning even. Her pale blonde hair, languid, deep green eyes and slender build are etched in my mind. Despite her admirable features, she tries very hard to promote a stern haughtiness. The tightly braided locks and conservative clothes are more suited to an older matron than a young, attractive lass like herself. Anyone who works so dutifully to disguise her true nature is clearly hurting on the inside.

I shake my head before taking a sip from my pint. I knew there was something off about her immediately— something timid and afraid—and I still managed to frighten her away with my careless words. Of course she should panic at the thought of traveling away from her home and accompanied by two strange men. How much worse if she knew there were actually *three* of us? Traveling alone with so many men is hardly ideal for any woman. But how to convince her we mean her no harm?

Well, no harm other than warming my bed at night, I think to myself.

"Ah, beer, exactly what I need!" Vaughn roars as he arrives at the table, sitting down hard enough to make the chair squeak.

"I figured as much," I reply, letting my thoughts about Ember Limus fall to the wayside while I push a pint in his direction. Aimes quietly takes his own seat on the other end of the table and begins nursing his beer.

Once Vaughn takes his first large gulp, I say, "Aimes informed you of our meeting with Ms. Limus?"

"Moaned about it, more like," Vaughn scoffs. "At least we know where to go next."

"True, but if Ms. Limus is correct, we'll face the same problem at the Wicked Lyre," I say.

Now that he has some alcohol in him, Aimes seems to relax. "I say we go to this tavern, find any ciphers there, copy them down and send them back to Ember."

"We've been over this, Aimes," I say impatiently, shaking my head. "Not only would that take far too long, but we'd have to ensure the map's safety in transit once it's decoded."

"And who knows how far this journey will take us?" Vaughn adds. "We could be at quite a distance, possibly even in hostile territory, while awaiting our next move."

"All right, all right!" Aimes replies defiantly. He takes another pull from his mug before adding. "So, what do we do? We can hardly force Ember to go with us. And even if we did, she could refuse to tell us what the cipher means, or worse, steer us into peril out of sheer spite."

"She doesn't strike me as the spiteful sort," I argue.

"Perhaps," Aimes chimes in after chugging down the last of his beer. "But we both know people do things they normally wouldn't do if their hands are forced."

By now, all our pints are spent and Vaughn waves to the barkeep for another round.

I look down at my now-empty mug as I bemoan the obstacles now facing us. "We shouldn't have frightened her by mentioning her accompanying us on this trip. We should have allowed her a bit of time to warm up to us. To make her believe—"

"We aren't wolves in sheeps' clothing?" Vaughn laughs.

"Speak for yourselves," Aimes responds. "I'm no wolf."

"No, you my lad, are the most stand-up, respectable man I've ever met," I answer.

"Aye," Vaughn says as he nods, then looks at me. "You and I… we're the wolves."

I chuckle and cheers to that (with my empty tankard) because I can't deny it.

Aimes shakes his head and chuckles. "My impression of Ember Limus is that she's scared of her own shadow. I don't think either of us ever stood a chance, wolf or sheep."

"If we don't do something soon, neither will Fantasia stand a chance," Vaughn reminds us in a dark tone. "The whispers I've been hearing lately claim that

Hassan has emerged from the broken seals. And now he's after the wand."

"Fuck," I exhale.

The round arrives and Vaughn waits until the barmaid leaves before continuing. "If Hassan finds the map and turns it over to Septimus, fucked is exactly what we'll be. The Seelie Princess will have no hope of defeating him once and for all."

"And she came so close to doing just that," I note with admiration. "The stories I've heard of Tinker's confrontation with the Unseelie King make me deeply regret not being there to witness it for myself. Or even to help strike the final blow."

"While it's true we might currently have the advantage," Aimes says, "the fact remains: once Septimus heals, he'll be hellbent on vengeance against Tinker. He'll punish her gravely for the insult."

"And it won't end there," Vaughn warns.

"Indeed not," Aimes agrees. "So we've no time to coddle our Ms. Limus."

"Then what do you suggest?" I reply, now at a loss.

Aimes purses his lips before saying, "Incentive."

I raise my chin at him. "Money did not suffice, so what do you suggest?"

"I don't yet know," he admits, stroking his chin while wiping the beer from his lips. "But everyone ultimately wants or needs something. I doubt our fair, Ms. Limus, is any exception."

"Fair is she?" Vaughn asks.

I look at him and raise my eyebrows to the ceiling. "Stunning is more like it." Vaughn looks to Aimes who simply nods, then he turns back to me. "Probably the most beautiful woman any of us has ever laid eyes on."

"Come now," Vaughn says, shaking his head.

"He's right," Aimes insists.

"The most beautiful and the most difficult," I finish on a sigh.

Vaughn gives a mirthless chuckle. "Well, stunningly beautiful or not, we need to figure out something soon."

I shake my head. "Why couldn't she just have made this easy by just saying yes?"

"Wishing alone won't make it so," Vaughn points out. "We need to convince her."

What kind of life did she have before that would make her so frightened and distrustful? I ask myself.

Putting the mug down, I look at Vaughn and say, "Follow her and figure out what makes her tick. I hardly need to add you must be quick about it because time is slipping through our fingers and has been."

"We'll start tomorrow," Aimes answers.

"Why not today?" I ask as I stand to leave.

Vaughn scoffs. "As if she'll emerge from whatever mousehole she crawled into before the next sunrise. She'll wait us out until she thinks we've given up."

"Which means she'll likely stay in that building where she works, if my initial reconnaissance is correct," Aimes says. "Guess we'll have to be more inventive."

I smile at both of them. "I would expect nothing less from either of you." I take one last pull from the mug and say my farewells. I leave the two of them to enjoy their evening. Tomorrow, they will be none the worse for wear and more than ready to attend to the matter at hand.

Then I step outside to join the evening throngs as I reflect upon Aimes and Vaughn. They make a good team, always working in sync. Yes, they are fine men to have by my side. Vaughn is an expert sellsword with experience in boobytraps. His skills as a battle tactician are unparalleled in any land. I'd always heard the legends that surrounded him long before I ever met him, though by the time we crossed paths, he'd retired to manage an apple orchard.

Reluctantly, Vaughn agreed to leave retirement and work for the palace, specifically, training my knights. In battle, he never hesitated to fight for the crown. His curly hair was nearly shoulder length when we met, but owing to an enemy attempting to use his long hair to his advantage and nearly slashing his throat, Vaughn now crops it short. To this day, the evidence of that attack is a heavy pink scar that stretches from one side of his neck to the other, easily visible against his sun-tanned skin. He also incurred a deep, gravelly voice from the damage inflicted on his windpipe.

Like Vaughn, Aimes is also on his second life. His first incarnation was a glass blower's apprentice. Under the tutelage of a superior weapon forger in the kingdom, his skills quickly surpassed those of his master. There were always rumors of Aimes possessing magic, though he, himself, has never acknowledged them, so I suppose they're untrue.

Regardless, Aimes's skill was hard-born and well earned, permanently displayed on his hands in the form of scars and burns common to his trade. The various splotches, craters and lines upon his hands and forearms make up a pattern that resembles a map, similar to the one Ms. Limus deciphered. Aimes wears his scars like a badge of honor, claiming to have learned from each one, mostly to respect hot items.

I consider once more what I intend to do regarding Ember Limus.

And I hate it from the bottom of my heart.

I know our lovely future companion doesn't deserve to be manipulated into traveling with us, but there are more important matters to consider than her feelings, unfortunately for her. If the map can save the realms, it will be worth the guilt I'm now suffering.

CHAPTER FOUR
EMBER

I have no idea how long I lie in bed.

But a glance at the clock tells me the time is nearly 6 PM. It will be dark soon, and while I don't like leaving the sanctity of my home, I haven't been to visit my mother and sister yet this week. And with my packed work schedule, there won't be any spare time after today. Thus, I need to get over my anxiety and be on my way.

It's not as though they want to see me any more than I want to see them, really. The silent accusation of *murderer!* is always in their eyes. But the fact is: I'm their only source of livelihood and they're entirely dependent on me, so these visits are important.

I sigh before climbing out of bed. From the bottom drawer, I pull out an old pair of pants and an equally old tunic. I feel the coarse fabric chafe against my skin as I slip the pants on. After donning a hooded cape— and trying not to think it resembles the prince's—I climb up the stairs to my office. I'm relieved to find everyone gone for the day. I slip out the front doors, locking them behind me before hurrying along the path that leads out of the city. The buildings eventually yield to the surrounding woods, and I find myself nearing my mother's house.

Given her poverty, people would be surprised to know that my mother is a descendant of dragon shifters. However, she is so far removed from the draconic bloodline that she lacks the ability to change her form. Her blood still retains one strictly familial trait though: the relentless need to hoard those things she considers "treasure." She shares that pleasure with my remaining sister, but not with me. My dragon legacy manifests as a strange, silvery sheen in my white-blonde hair, as well as an underlying scaly pattern in my skin. But the pattern is extremely difficult to see.

Unlike her draconic forebears, my mother hoards trash and other useless items. Where a true dragon would dwell exclusively around gold or jewels, her home overflows with worthless junk. Yet, she doesn't view it the same way and happily forages through trash to retrieve more and more rubbish. Sometimes she'll stumble on an item that might be worth at least something, but such objects are rare. Truly, a jeweled locket is no more valuable to her than a hideous, malformed vase, some poor soul's pathetic attempt at turning pottery.

There's simply no rhyme or reason for her choices and my sister is exactly the same. Thus, their home is brimming with everything from stacks of old newspapers and magazines, to other people's trophies, to crystals that possess no magic. Piles of random clothing and material scraps fill all the corners and cover the furniture.

I had hoped they'd stop hoarding after poor Talia was literally buried alive beneath the clutter. But no!

They felt compelled to replace anything that was taken after Talia's body was removed. My mother's madness demands treatment, but I can ill-afford the sort of help she needs. And my sister isn't much better—she does whatever Mother tells her to do. With each passing day, I fear my mother's sickness is finding new life within my sister. Together, the two of them are wasting away within their empire of rubbish.

Such thoughts occupy my mind when I arrive at Mother's door. I take a deep breath and strip off my cloak, folding it over the crook of my elbow. Then, I knock three times before opening the door. When I step inside, the smell is foul, hitting me almost as hard as a physical blow. I can feel my heart racing as I step across the threshold. The clutter rises up around me, like the great rock walls of some deep cavern. I have to close my eyes and steel myself against the sudden urge to turn around and flee. I attribute my absolute hatred for anything disorderly to this house and my mother's sickness.

Every time I come here, it seems as though the configuration of the maze adopts a different pattern. Ignoring my reflexive panic, I carefully make my way through the piles and stacks of junk.

As usual, I look up for guidance. Like stars to a sailor, the familiar layout of the ceiling is my only source of navigation through the columns of trash. It matters not what shape the clutter has taken. Every beam and nick above will guide me through.

The smell grows worse as I approach the bedroom, shared by my mother and sister. I don't have to bother with opening the door because it's already forced open and hidden behind a seven-foot pile of refuse.

Catching sight of Mother and Marzella sitting on the bed, I temporarily forget the smell, because I'm so completely shocked by their appearance. Both have been severely beaten, bruises running up and down their bodies.

"What happened to you?" I gasp, carefully stepping over a knee-high pile of books.

"Mother tried to steal something from one of the merchants outside the castle walls," Marzella replies in a flat tone. "He caught her and beat both of us."

She speaks as though this beating is just a commonplace occurrence. For all I know, it could be. But I've never seen them look this bad. The closer I get, the more bruises I see. I can only guess how bad the beatings actually were.

"Triple goddess, preserve us." I'm having a hard time breathing in this pervasive odor. How do they stand it? It's so terrible, I can scarcely pay attention to their bruised and wounded faces.

"It's all right, Ember," Marzella replies, letting some warmth into her voice. "We're all right." Mother says nothing, but stares off into the distance.

"She doesn't seem all right," I counter, pointing at her. "Does she need a doctor?"

"She's fine," my sister tells me. "Don't overreact and besides, you know as well as I do that we can't afford a doctor and no doctor would come here to begin with."

She's correct on both accounts.

"I can't understand…" I begin, but Marzella interrupts.

"There's nothing to understand." Her eyes turn toward the bag in my hand. "What is that?"

Despite my growing panic and worry that the walls of trash are going to collapse around us yet again, I manage to hold out the bag I packed before leaving home. Marzella accepts it and then takes the pouch containing some of the money Mr. Padmoore, *Aimes*, gave me. If I'm careful, it will be enough for them to survive for quite a while. My sister takes both without comment.

Finally, the stench drives me to my absolute limit. "I... I have to go now."

And such is the truth, because the last time I was here, I waited too long and suffered an attack of sorts— a panic attack, Cecilia termed it and I suppose she was correct because such was what it felt like—absolute and sheer panic.

Not waiting for a response, I stumble back towards the door. The trusty ceiling keeps me on course until my hand falls on the blessed knob that promises freedom. Never once do I hear either Marzella nor my mother tell me goodbye or thank me. But, no matter. I pull the door shut and throw my cloak back over my shoulders, then I run toward the forest path that leads back to the city.

A few paces later, I begin to calm as the fresh air rejuvenates me. Gradually, my pace slows and my thoughts clear enough to consider what just happened and why I suddenly felt the need to escape. Simply put, the claustrophobia was insufferable. It wasn't even the smell that was the worst of it—it was the fear of everything falling down around me again. It was the memories of Talia's dead stare. It was… everything.

This day is truly turning out to be dreadful and easily one of the worst I've had in a while. I was already stressed after the meeting with Aimes and the prince. And piling on the situation at home—it was just too much to bear. All at once, I realize tears are rolling down my face. For whom? Mother? Marzella? Myself?

I wipe my tears away and continue on the path that leads through the forest and back to the city. I'm pleased to see that I'm very close to the city walls. My safe quarters are just a few paces away.

Slipping inside my building, I retrieve one of the laundry bags I keep outside my office. They're hidden beneath the seat of a storage bench for just this purpose. I take off the cape and drop it inside one of the bags, then leave it on the bench with a note to send it to the washerwoman. Then I step inside my office, strip off my dirty clothes and hastily drop them into the waste basket. I set the receptacle outside the door for the cleaning staff to empty. After locking my office door, I hurry down to my private quarters.

I take a long bath and put on a clean nightgown before I sit on my bed to ponder the situation with Mother. She and Marzella simply can't keep living the way they have been. The day will come when they're buried to death by their hoarding, such as Talia was. While I can't leave them to die there, I also can't keep visiting them in all that disgusting filth—my reaction to it today is proof enough. No, it wasn't as bad as my reaction last week, but it came close.

They need help, certainly, whatever the cost. But how in the world can I help them on such limited funds?

CHAPTER SIX
VAUGHN

I'm eager to get started on our journey.

Patience has never been my strong suit and yet, Aimes wants to take his time where tracking Ember Limus is concerned. I, however, don't.

Thus, when Aimes returned, I told him I was going for a walk to clear my head. I'm not certain if he believed me, but he certainly didn't stop me.

And it wasn't a complete lie—I *did* go for a walk. Only, that walk happened to be trailing a certain blonde-haired, uptight woman in a cloak. At dusk, I watched for our target outside her work building. Even though Aimes assured us she lives there, I still find it strange, as I've never come across a woman who made her home in her place of work.

When I saw her slip out under the cloak of darkness, I reminded myself it is always a bad idea to bet against Aimes's ability to ferret out information. He is always correct. Always.

Regardless, I followed her at a distance, tracking her from the city and onto the forest path that led to a decaying house in the middle of nowhere. Aimes didn't mention this place in his scouting report... and I wonder who on earth could live here?

Now, I find myself listening from a side window as Ember visits the residents. From the windows, I can see the horrible mess inside. I'm shocked when I discover the older resident is Ember's mother! The other woman—called Marzella—favors both Ember and the mother, so I speculate that she must be Ember's sister. Suddenly, much of Ember's peculiarities begin to make sense. If this is an example of the way in which she was raised… it's no wonder she's as peculiar as Aimes and Blake say she is.

I watch Ember hand her sister a bag and a coin pouch before her nerves begin to shatter. She nearly catches me spying when she barrels wildly out the front door, in what appears to be a panicked run back through the forest and towards the city. I consider following her again, but frankly, I'm more curious about this place and the people who live here. They might have the answer in getting Ember to cooperate with us.

And cooperate with us, she must. For the sake of all Fantasia.

Despite their visitor's hasty exit, the two women remain sitting on the bed, eating two of the fresh apples from the bag Ember gave them. When they finish, they toss the cores into a heap of rotting trash in the corner. I'm repulsed just thinking about how awful the smell must be inside.

Still, haven't I been in worse places? I think to myself. Sure, but only because I was fulfilling my duty. To willingly live this way is nothing short of madness.

I slip away from the window and step onto the porch. I've learned all I can from watching The time has come for action and I am a man who is much more comfortable with action. I knock on the front door, using three raps just as Ember did.

Marzella answers the door, looking at me suspiciously through the narrow opening. Up close, she's a rather plain girl and her appearance is all the more concerning, given her two black eyes, a puffy bruise on her right cheek and a split lip.

"Can I help you?" she asks with an audibly distrustful voice. She shifts her arms and I see additional bruises on both of them.

"Yes, I came here with Ember, your sister," I lie with ease, as fabrication is an art form I have mastered.

"With Ember?" she repeats, eyeing me narrowly.

I nod and give her a practiced smile. "She asked me to come back and apologize for her leaving so suddenly."

"She did?" the younger woman replies, unimpressed. "That doesn't sound like Ember."

"Oh, it's quite true. She cares very deeply about you and your mother."

The mention of the mother makes Marzella bristle a little. "Why would she bring *you* here? You hardly seem like someone she'd associate with... for one, you're a man."

My turn to bristle. "She wouldn't associate with me because I'm a man?"

"That and you're untidy."

Granted, I do have quite a slovenly appearance with my shirt untucked and the laces of my boots undone. And, it's true that I haven't washed these pants in a week or so, but isn't this accusation a bit ridiculous? I make a point of looking into the rubbish pile she calls home. "It would appear you're far less tidy."

"Probably," Marzella replies with a note of venom. "But the fact remains that Ember isn't fond of dirt or disorder, no matter where it comes from." She glares up at me then. "Who are you again?"

"Oh, no one important," I respond with what I hope is a handsome smile and, yet, I feel quite self-conscious now that she's pointed out my slovenly habits.

"And yet you arrived here with my sister, or so you claim?"

I nod. "Ember asked me to escort her through the woods."

"But you didn't escort her back to Sweetland, to her home?"

"Not yet. She's waiting nearby because… she just needed a few minutes to… collect herself. You understand."

Marzella gives me a sneer. "Of course," she spits, contempt dripping off her lips. "She had another panic attack, I'll wager." I start to respond, but she takes a step forward and holds a long and bony finger in front of my face. "If you think I care about those silly attacks of hers, I've seen them my whole life, so think again."

It's obvious I'm not getting anywhere with this awful woman, so I try a different tact. "Might I have a brief word with your mother?"

Marzella's eyes grow even more suspicious. "For what reason?"

"Ember is concerned about your mother's… *state* and asked me to check on her. I promise I won't be long."

The flames in Marzella's eyes dull back to their former sullen apathy. "You can try, but she's not in a speaking mood today. She's been quiet since we got in a row with that merchant at the market."

"What merchant?"

She points at her black eye. "The one who did this."

A deep, familiar rage starts to take hold of my heart. "A man did that to you?" I ask, my voice several octaves deeper.

"Even worse, to my mother."

While I've been faking my feelings for the whole conversation, there is no denying the fury building up inside me. "Men have no business hitting women." It's the only true statement I've made thus far.

"He would disagree," Marzella says with casual resignation.

"Give me his name."

She looks surprised, but as soon as I let her peek into the anger boiling inside me through the ire seeping out of my eyes, she nods.

"Peter Barstow," she says.

"What sort of merchant is he?"

"He sells healing crystals by the castle."

"Healing? Ironic," I reply. "Now, about that word with your mother...?"

Although she's not exactly warmer than before, Marzella does step back and wave me inside.

"Well, come in then."

Upon stepping foot inside the hovel, I'm struck by two things—first, I don't understand how it's humanly possible to fit the amount of... stuff within this space such that they have. And, second, the smell hits me like a battering ram. A rancid mixture of decayed food, unwashed bodies and dirt—it's every bit as vile as I feared. Holding my breath, Marzella leads me through a tunnel of trash and I sincerely doubt I'd be able to find my way back out again.

When we reach the bedroom, the mother is still sitting on the edge of the bed as she was earlier and staring into space, er, I think it would be more fitting to say, staring into trash.

"Hello," I start, but there is no response. "I'm Ember's friend." Still nothing.

I spend several minutes attempting to speak to the mother. The most I get is a glance in my direction from two empty eyes, devoid of any thought or feeling. Finally, I give up and make a hasty retreat to the front porch, gasping for fresh air. Marzella is close behind me. Once there, I ask her, "Are you sure she's all right, your mother?"

"Yes," Marzella says. "She had fits like this before the beating. She'll snap out of it when she's ready."

"I hope so," I respond, meaning every word. "I best be going. It's a long walk back to the city."

"Tell Ember the money and food she left won't last long," Marzella calls after me as I turn to leave.

"I will relay your message," I assure her over my shoulder as I'm suddenly pleased I made this little trip. It's just as I assumed—Ember is supporting her mother and sister and doing so on a salary in which she can most undoubtedly barely support herself. And that is her Achilles heel. Unfortunately for her (or fortunately, depending how you look at it) we will use that weakness to our ends.

"Good night."

The moment I enter the treeline, I suck in as much clean air as my lungs can hold. Though I'm grateful for the cool breeze blowing across my skin, I fear I've absorbed the stench from inside that wretched house and I wonder if I'll ever empty the awful odor from my nostrils. Small wonder why Ember was so distraught when she left. From what I can gather, she cares for her family, but can only do so much.

It's exactly the kind of leverage we need!

The following morning, I discuss my findings with Blake and Aimes. Of course, I assume Aimes will be cross with me for getting started without him, but he isn't just cross, he complains about it excessively.

It helps when Blake tells him, "You may recall that I advocated haste last night, Aimes?"

"Yes, but I wish Vaughn had thought to include me," Aimes pouts as he shoots me a glare before returning his insistent expression to Blake. "Is that not also part of my duties?"

"Oh, leave it be, man," I grumble. "Now that we know what motivates our clever girl, we need to figure out how to use it."

Aimes rubs his forehead. "Well, I doubt she'll let Blake or me anywhere near her after what happened in the rock garden. She'll be wary of us and then some."

"Well, one of the benefits of being a prince is that I can always *insist* she meet with me," Blake points out.

"Which, with respect, would only make the situation worse," Aimes counters.

Blake glances at me, and I shrug. "He's right. If you're trying to win her trust, that's not the way to do it."

"And that's why you, Vaughn, should meet with her in our place," Aimes concludes.

I'm not sure what he's getting at. "What do you mean?"

Aimes begins to tick his reasons off on his fingers. "Ember has yet to see you, you are persuasive in your own *blunt* way, and the fact that you've spoken with her family means you can anticipate how she'll react." He bounces his index finger between himself and Blake. "Unlike either of us." I look at Blake, who nods his agreement.

Yet, what they aren't taking into account is that I'm me and they are them. "I'm not nearly charming enough or smart enough to persuade someone like her to join us on our quest." I glare at them both. "Remember, I'm usually the brawn of this outfit, and that's it."

Blake's smile tells me he knows something I don't. Putting a hand on my shoulder, he says, "You were both charming and smart enough to interrogate Ms. Limus's family, Vaughn. You can do the same with her."

I make my way to Ember's building around noon. En route, I take one small detour to the castle. After all, I have a promise to see to and a reputation to maintain. In no time at all, I find a certain merchant named Peter Barstow who deals in healing crystals.

Naturally, I kick the ever-loving shit out of him as I tell him if he ever lays a finger on another woman, I'll return and beat him worse than I already have. He seems to take the warning to heart. Once my fists begin to hurt, I decide I've walloped him enough and in my escape, I somehow manage to avoid the castle guards.

All in all, it's a good outing.

But, my pleased feelings begin to fade when I contemplate the next visit on my list. Ember Limus doesn't deserve to be manipulated, but I have to do so, all the same. I hope Barstow's thrashing, which he so richly earned, does some small measure to balance the scales.

###

"Ember Limus, I'd like to speak with you for a moment," I say while standing outside Ember's office door.

She looks up, startled by my voice, perhaps even more so by my appearance. It's a common reaction to those who see my battle-weathered face and the hideous scar that spans my neck. Then again, maybe she's not used to people who can so easily slip past the receptionist at the desk.

"Who... Who are you and what do you need to speak to me about?" she asks, her voice soft and nervous.

Now that the moment has arrived, it suddenly feels much more difficult to do what I came here to do. Steeling myself, I begin, "I won't take up much of your time. I've come to make you a simple offer."

She looks nervously at the hallway as though she doesn't want to invite me into her office.

"I'm happy to remain across the room from you if it makes you feel better," I offer.

She doesn't say anything but swallows hard as she waves me into her office but doesn't shut the door. I suppose that's smart. Once she sits down behind her desk, she asks, "An offer of what kind, exactly?"

I hesitate. Gods, but she looks so fragile. Her silvery white hair cascades over her left shoulder in a tight braid, and her wide green eyes are full of curiosity. She's beautiful—just as Aimes and Blake said she was. It wasn't that I doubted them, but last night I didn't get a good look at her while she was wearing her cape in the dark. But, looking at her now, it almost seems like they downplayed her beauty.

Regardless, I don't want to do this. I really don't. But I have to. I take in a deep breath and slowly let it out. "I know about your mother and sister."

Some of the fire I saw in Marzella's eyes is reflected in Ember's emerald ones and the fear that was there moments earlier fades slightly. Her eyes narrow on me.

"What of them?"

"I know they need help, your mother especially, but you can't afford to get such help for them, even with that healthy payment Aimes gave you yesterday for decoding the map."

Her eyes go from fright to anger at the very mention of Aimes.

"How dare you!" she says in her soft voice and immediately stands up from behind her desk.

"Sit down," I say with steely conviction, pointing my finger downward for more emphasis. I use the same tone on disobedient recruits and it has the same effect on her as it does on them. Her eyes go wide and she sits immediately.

Her breathing grows short, sporadic, and panicky. If I'm going to make my pitch, it has to be now. "I don't have time to argue with you," I say, lowering myself to sit at eye level with her or close to it. I easily have a head in height over her. "Here is what I—what *we* are offering you and we don't expect you to turn us down." I take a breath, wondering if she'll argue, but she just sits there and looks up at me with fear in her wide eyes. "If you accompany us on our journey to find the map and decipher it and any others we recover, Prince Nonpareil will take both Marzella and your mother to the palace and place them under the protection of the royal guard."

"How do you know my sister's name?" she asks between her labored breathing, her eyes now back to narrowed and angry. "And how do you know about my family?"

"Does it matter?"

She purses her lips and stares at me and I'm once again drawn in by her beauty. She has a stunning figure, a perfect face. I can only imagine what her lips might taste like, should she allow anyone to ever sample them. But, according to Aimes and Blake, she's cold—frigid.

"And my... my family doesn't need protection from the royal guard," she stubbornly replies.

"They will if someone who shouldn't discovers the gift you have for ciphers," I warn her. She immediately looks up at me then, alarm in her gaze. "Need I remind you we are in a war?"

"I'm aware."

"Then you must also be aware that your skills in wartime are critical. And as soon as word spreads, people will be coming for you from all over. But, you already know that which is why you keep your family at arm's length... to protect them."

She wavers but remains defiant. "And the prince will do a better job protecting them?"

"Without a doubt."

"I'm not convinced."

"Regardless, that's not the end of the offer," I continue as I regain her curiosity again. "Your family will live in luxury at the palace. Their every want will be seen to. And…a healer will be brought to mend your mother's damaged mind."

A glimmer of hope flickers in her eyes. "Is that even possible?"

"The prince has access to the finest healers in the land," I assure her. "So you tell me."

She starts frowning, but I can see hope growing stronger in her eyes. "And in return, all the prince wants is for me to accompany him on this little treasure hunt for the map?"

"Yes. But the price of care for your family will be the successful recovery of the artifact we seek."

The hostility returns to her eyes. "You mean my family won't be—"

"You have to earn the right for such lavish considerations." When she refuses to budge, I know I have no choice but to tell her the next part. "Furthermore, if you refuse, the prince could evict your family from their hovel and have it demolished."

"This is extortion!" she says, standing up as her anger pours from her. Even though she doesn't raise her voice, her shoulders shake with her own outrage. She doesn't seem quite so frigid now—no, now she seems alive, angered with fiery passion.

"Dammit, this isn't personal to you! We are in the midst of war!" I shout at her, rising to my feet and slamming the desk with my fist. I blow a breath out before saying, "Don't you understand? If Morningstar wins, everything you know and take for granted will go up in smoke... and that's if you're lucky."

Not meeting my eyes, Ember starts pacing behind her desk. "This isn't my battle."

"This is *everyone's* battle," I say in a softer tone. "All we ask is that you complete this one task, something you obviously *can* do and might even enjoy."

She stops her pacing to look at me. "You have no right to bring my family into this."

"Were it my family, I might agree. But we have to do what we have to and time is running out." I stand up and walk around the desk, towards her. She takes a step back and I can see she's afraid of me. Good. Let her be afraid so she can understand the threat we face—her just as much as the rest of us. All of Fantasia, for that matter.

"Shall I tell you what's going to happen if Morningstar wins?" I ask.

She doesn't back down, so I take another step nearer her, almost unable to keep the words from my tongue. "I know you fear men, Ember," I say, my voice low and heated. "And Morningstar will know that too and once he finds you, he'll bend you over that desk and take what he wants from you! Or he'll make you the property of whomever he decides to sell you to!"

Her hand shoots out and upward, but I'm far too quick. I grab her wrist before her slap lands. Despite the fear on her face, she's more defiant than ever. God and goddess! She's so small, so fragile. Suddenly, at the thought of her in Morningstar's hands, a spire of anger builds within me.

Now that she's closer, I can see how extraordinarily beautiful she truly is. An almost unnatural perfection, as if she isn't completely human. No, she's not human, is she? Yet, for the life of me, I can't figure out what sort of magical half breed she might be. Still, I'm here to do a job, not to admire her or trace her family tree.

I lower her arm, still holding her wrist in my hand. "I advise you not to try to slap me again," I tell her quietly. "And if you do, put a lot more power behind it than that."

She jerks her hand free before walking back toward her desk. Leaning forward for a moment, her head is down so I can't see her face, but I sense the turmoil inside her. I wait silently, giving her a chance to sort out her thoughts. I'm not ashamed to admire the view she presents to me, I must admit.

"Fine," she says, raising her head. "Tell *Prince Blake Nonpareil* and *Mr. Aimes Padmoore* that I accept their unfair offer."

"This is the best decision you can make, for your family and for those fighting Morningstar," I assure her. "You won't regret it."

Her eyes are stern and cold. "Get out of my office."

I know better than to linger. Once I stroll out the door, I nod to the imp at the reception desk—who looks surprised—before exiting the front doors.

As I blend into the crowd outside, I reflect on our meeting. It went as well as I could have expected. Aimes will be quite displeased by my methods, but what can I say? I'm a direct man and so I was… direct. Regardless, Ember will keep her end of the bargain. All we need to do is survive long enough to keep ours.

A smile crosses my face as I consider her great beauty and fire. For some reason, the image of a huge ice dragon flashes across my mind, but I dismiss the vision quickly. Ember is no dragon. No, she couldn't even turn herself into a drake.

Even so, I wish I'd kissed her while I had the chance. It's a strange thought, but one I ponder all the same. There was something about her fire, her anger and how it was trapped in that little mouse of a woman that makes me… *want her*. Yes, that's what this is. I want to fuck the anger out of her—to see how alive she'd become in my hands.

I really am a sick bastard.

CHAPTER SEVEN
AIMES

The journey toward our destination feels like a funeral procession.

Ms. Limus is naturally silent and sullen, her resentment toward us casting a dark, gray cloud over everything. Despite the serious nature of our work, our journeys in the past were always quite light-spirited, filled with jokes and tales aplenty.

Now, none of us are speaking.

Our collective guilt over what we've forced upon this poor girl is evident. Indulging in the slightest joy under such circumstances would be in bad taste. It doesn't help that she's so delicate and vulnerable. After the first day, I can safely say she regards us with loathing, bordering on outright hatred.

The trail we ride is dirty and dusty, and Ms. Limus struggles with both, owing to her condition. It's a peculiar condition—one that causes her to constantly need to cleanse herself. Thus, it is fortuitous that we are beside the river, which allows her a place to bathe with each stop. Perhaps "bathe" is too light a word. Instead, she scrubs herself to the bone, as if nothing less can remove the filth from her skin. She also washes her clothing every evening before hanging each item up to dry. While her clothing dries, she sleeps in an unflattering robe. The three of us sleep beneath the stars, but she takes her rest inside a canvas tent she erects herself, refusing to allow us to assist with it.

It's so quiet out here.

Even the slightest noise is audible for miles and I wish it weren't so, because every night, Ember sobs in her tent. It's heartbreaking for each of us, but none of us is man enough to comfort her. She wouldn't allow it, anyway. I find myself repeatedly wondering if perhaps there was a better way to have secured her assistance.

As the sun sets this night, I decide I've had enough. And if neither Vaughn nor the prince will speak to her, then I will.

Vaughn is cooking, and the prince is writing in his journal as Ember heads toward the river, no doubt to bathe or wash her clothing. Watching her leave, I hurry to my feet to catch up to her.

Despite my haste, by the time I approach, her outer layer of clothing is lying on the river bank and she heads for the water, still clad in her very conservative undergarments. This stretch of the river has much steeper banks than our previous encampments, along with jagged, steep rocks. But she seems oblivious to the peril, so hellbent as she is on bathing.

Since I lack Vaughn's talent for stealth, I'm certain she sees me approaching. Nevertheless I call out to her. "Be careful, Ember. It's a treacherous climb down."

"I don't care," she replies, sliding down the first rock with stark indifference.

"Please, just stop a moment," I growl, frustrated as I continue toward her. "Let me help you."

Surely no bath is worth such peril, I think as I reach her, near the edge of the craggy descent.

"I don't need your help to climb down a few rocks, Mr. Padmoore," she snaps. Since our reacquaintance, she hasn't called me by my first name and I'm certain that fact is intended to place more distance between us.

"Please, as I've told you... call me Aimes."

She hasn't continued down the path further, but that's because she's still trying to figure out the safest route. And she also doesn't respond to my comment. I notice with encouragement that I'm closing in on her.

"There's a better way."

She lifts an eyebrow at me. "To climb the rocks?"

"To clean yourself," I clarify. "I have certain *gifts*... magical in nature, that will aid you in cleansing your body without having to scrub your skin off."

She seems unimpressed. "The river's done a good job so far."

"How can you be sure the water isn't tainted?"

She glances down at the water and then looks back at me, her eyes rounding with doubt. She then seems to remember she's dressed only in her undergarments and blushes profusely as she wraps one of her arms across her breasts. Not that doing so matters all that much because her clothing is so starched and heavy, I couldn't see through it even if I tried. And I'm not since I'm a gentleman.

She finally finds her voice. "How can these gifts of yours cleanse me?"

"I really wish I could explain, but I'm afraid I can only show you, which… of course, requires your trust."

She glares at me. "Why should I trust someone who's holding my family hostage?"

I wince. "For what it's worth, I knew Vaugn's was the wrong approach, and I advised Blake against taking it."

"Why should I believe a word that comes out of your mouth?"

"Because I want to help you and you have my word as… as a gentleman."

She reaches the edge of the rock and stares at me with seething venom, but says nothing. Her eyes give me a cold appraisal and I search for any other topic of conversation. Strangely, Ember beats me to it.

"I notice you never get dirty even though we are on this trail day in and out and the others are covered with dust and grime... do you use your own gifts?"

"I do," I answer and give her a smile, which she ignores. "I can share them with you if you wish."

She looks down at the river and then up at me. The blatant calculation never leaves her eyes, making it difficult to guess what she's thinking. Then she abruptly climbs back onto the bank proper.

"Very well. How does it work?"

"First, I… I must touch your bare skin."

"My *bare* skin?"

"Your arm will suffice," I say quickly, not wanting her to think I'm trying to get a thrill at her expense.

She nods and reaches out, offering her arm only after pushing her nightgown up to her elbow. Reaching for her hand, I focus on her skin. I'm intrigued by how smooth it is to the touch, like porcelain. The more I study her, the more I notice her skin isn't just porcelain, but there's a slight pattern—as if someone had pushed a checkered board against her and her skin had adopted the pattern. Vaughn must have been correct when he told us she wasn't entirely human. But what could the other half of her heritage be? Siren? Dragon? Merfolk?

A sudden gasp from her jostles me from my trailing thoughts. I look up to see her wide eyes focused on me as her silver hair falls loose and flows with the breeze, as clean as the rest of her, thanks to my magic.

"How did you do that?" she gasps in wonder. "I feel as if I've just enjoyed a hot bath." She looks down at herself and rubs the skin of her arms experimentally. "Cleaner, actually."

"I do not understand it entirely," I admit with a shrug. "It was as if one day my magic simply emerged and it has remained all this time."

She studies me and there's curiosity in her gaze. "What limits your power?"

I pull my head back and frown. "That's the first time anyone has ever asked me that question."

She shrugs her slight shoulders. "All power has limitations. It's only a question of what."

I'm as attracted to her beautiful mind as I am to her lovely face and body. "Well, in my case, I have to touch an object's pure essence."

"Such as when you just touched my arm?" I nod as she continues. "This is all quite fascinating," she says, bending down to pick up her clothes. The flesh between my legs twitches as I catch sight of her shapely backside. When she rises with her clothes in her arms, she asks, "Do you mind cleaning my clothing?"

"Not at all, Ms. Limus," I reply, stretching my fingers over them.

She surprises me when she says after a few beats. "You may call me Ember."

I smile at her. The clothes are easier to clean than a human body and faster. She thanks me, which prompts me to ask, "Why does dirt bother you so much?"

Her face grows glum. "I'm sure Vaughn described the state of my mother's home."

I have no wish to hurt or insult her, so I merely nod. She goes on to say, "It's been that way all my life—dirt and chaos surrounding me." That fire I glimpsed earlier comes back into her eyes. "No matter how many times I tried to clean it, Mother wouldn't allow me. She feared I might destroy some of her precious 'treasures'." Then her expression settles once more.

"Then you feel out of control when you or your possessions aren't clean," I conclude.

"I suppose that's obvious, isn't it?"

I give the matter some thought and nod. She breathes in deeply and then does something she hasn't this entire trip—she smiles at me. "Thank you for your kindness."

I nod. "I'll... make a deal with you."

Immediately, her eyes narrow. "What sort of deal?"

"If you keep my magic strictly between us, I'm happy to clean you whenever we rest for the night."

She gives me a doubtful look. "The others don't know about your magic?"

"I don't fully understand it, so I haven't been eager to share it. Sometimes I wonder if it's truly a curse."

"Why would you think it a curse?"

I shrug. "I don't know where it came from."

She nods. "It doesn't seem like a curse to me." Then she clears her throat. "I'm happy to keep your secret, but won't it quickly become obvious to the others?"

"Well, I suppose we can... sneak away once they become occupied with something else?"

She looks as though I just offered her the prince's entire treasury. "You would do that for me? Risk the upset of your comrades, your friends?"

"I would." I breathe in deeply. "As I told you, Ember, we're not horrible men. Our only concern is for the well-being of the king—" Footsteps approach from the direction of the camp. "I hear someone coming," I finish anxiously.

I hand her clean clothes back to her. "Once you're dressed, come eat something with us, will you?"

"As you please, Mr. Padmoore," she says.

No more than three paces from the clearing, I run into the others coming through a bay of nearby trees.

"There you are," Vaughn says with one eyebrow cocked at me. "And just what are you doing all the way out here?"

I cross my arms. "Nothing important."

His eyes are amused. "You wouldn't happen to be spying on our sour companion, would you?"

"Of course not," I scoff. "What sort of cad do you take me for?"

"Do you really want an honest answer?"

Realizing Vaughn won't let the subject go, I respond. "If you must know, I was over in the brush taking a… a shit. Satisfied?"

He moves away from the clearing, shaking his head. "Gods, as if I want to know the details of your bowel movements. I was coming to let you know dinner is ready. I'd tell Ember, but I don't want to interrupt her in her… ministrations."

"Oh, and how would *you* know she's busy with *ministrations* if *you* aren't spying on her?"

"Anyone within earshot can hear that girl bathing in the water every chance she gets. Now, do you want to eat or not?"

I nod. "I do."

At his wave, I follow him back to camp. Already, I'm having doubts regarding whether I did the right thing. Hard to know if showing Ember my magic was a big mistake. But, what's done can't be undone.

CHAPTER EIGHT
BLAKE

Vaughn and Aimes emerge from the bushes as I finish roasting the rabbits I killed earlier. It's not a huge meal, but it's the best I can do for tonight. As I watch them, Vaughn teases Aimes about something, but before they come within earshot, he stops. That piques my curiosity. Aimes looks sheepish, so I know whatever they were talking about involves him.

A moment later, Ember appears, looking strangely less... *angry* than usual. I notice her clothes are every bit as spotless as her complexion. And, strangely enough, her clothing is the same she was wearing earlier today, so the fact that it's quite spotless should be impossible. And, interestingly enough, the same goes for Aimes.

How very... peculiar.

There's definitely something going on, but I can't quite put my finger on it.

"So, Ms. Limus," I say over the fire. "Have you discovered a new secret for eradicating trail dirt?"

"I suppose you could say as much," she replies and there's something in her manner I haven't seen before—something haughty, perhaps? No, it doesn't seem to be quite that—it's more as if she knows something I don't. For whatever reason, her candor causes the sudden desire to rip off her immaculately clean clothes so I can show her what truly getting dirty looks like. The feelings and thoughts are much too stimulating to my loins, and I turn away.

"Well, we best eat and get some sleep," I say, casting a meaningful glance to the starry sky. "Daylight comes early and we've still a long way to go."

"Do we ever," Vaughn grumbles as I offer him half a rabbit. "If I didn't know better, I'd swear we were spinning in one big circle." Aimes tears off half another rabbit for Ember. Unlike previous evenings, she seems almost eager to eat tonight. I can't fathom what might have changed her and shaken her out of her misery.

Were it anyone else, I'd assume Aimes had taken her to bed and within an inch of her life. His shy exterior aside, or perhaps due to it, Aimes is quite popular with the fairer sex. But I can't believe a prudish maid like Ember would allow such intimacy. Still, something must have happened between the two of them—I can tell as much because Ember chooses to sit beside him and as they eat, they cast glances at each other.

I realize all at once that I'm spending far too much time speculating about this silly subject. Who cares if Aimes bedded her? What does that subject matter to me?

Because I want to bed her, I answer myself. *Badly.*

Irritated with myself as well as the situation, I eat my share of rabbit and say goodnight. Taking a blanket to lie beneath a nearby tree, I roll up my outer coat to make a pillow under my head.

I always take a long time to surrender to sleep. So it's no surprise I find myself eavesdropping on the conversation between Vaughn, Aimes and occasionally, Ember as they talk by the fire. Ember is much quieter than they are. She seems warmer too. Well, at least she is with them, or *him*. Having threatened her entire family with destitution if she refused us, I am clearly not her favorite of the three of us. Yes, the words might have come from Vaughn, but we all know who issued the order. Me. Truly, why would she want anything to do with me after that?

I push those thoughts out of my head and roll onto my side, turning away from them. It takes a long time but eventually, I sleep.

We awaken before dawn and return to the trail. After traveling all morning, we reach a secluded spot where it's safe enough to stop to rest and eat. I look at Ember as I note how dirty she's become along the way. I can tell she's bothered by it, too, which doesn't bode well for the rest of the day. Usually by sundown, she becomes sullen and fidgety. Much to my surprise, she isn't upset now.

I pull out the rations of dried meat from my pack, which I offer the others, and notice when Ember takes her share, she says, "Aimes, if you'll assist me, we can find some berries and other wild edibles to eat with the dried meat."

"Of course," Aimes replies, following her like a loyal dog toward a nearby wooded area.

Once they're out of sight—and hopefully earshot too—Vaughn growls, "He must be fucking her."

"Hardly," I scoff. "She's as frigid as a lake."

"Gods and goddesses, man, look!" Vaughn realizes to whom he's talking and holds up his hands. "Forgive me, Your Highness, I forget my place."

"Oh, save that for the court, Vaughn," I reply, putting my hand on his shoulder. "Out here, my title means as much as my last bowel movement."

Vaughn chuckles, but then starts nodding again. "You're deluding yourself if you think the two of them aren't… *involved*. It's the only explanation for the drastic change in her behavior."

I continue to chew my jerky. If Aimes *is* fucking her, more power to him. At least one of us is getting perks from the lovely Ms. Limus. I ignore the jealous twinge that immediately sours my mood. To the winner go the spoils, I suppose. In that particular arena, titles are no better than they are on the open road.

Staying busy, I can't wait to see if Aimes and Ember have managed to scavenge anything good. It gets old eating nothing but tough meat day in and out. The rabbit last night was nice, but a rare treat. Our overwhelming need for haste doesn't allow enough time to hunt for food.

Aimes and Ember return with a small pouch of sweet blackberries and a bit of watercress they've found by the river. Vaughn and I are visibly glad for the improvement in our daily fare, but I can't help noticing how clean Ember looks. She was filthy when they walked away. There's no way she could have bathed, cleaned her clothes and put herself back together with dry hair and a stiff collar so quickly.

She takes her meal with Vaughn, who seems eager to chat her up. He probably hopes to get some of whatever she's giving to Aimes. Vaughn has a gruff bluntness that most women find attractive. I disregard the fresh pang of jealousy and taste the watercress leaves before chewing them up.

Then, with one eyebrow raised, I ask Aimes, "What in the nine hells is going on between you two?"

"Whatever do you mean?" Aimes responds, his nervous look betraying the innocent façade.

"I mean, how did Ember get clean so quickly after half a day's ride?"

When Aimes sighs, I notice Ember is somewhat startled. Between their two reactions, I'm definitely onto something. I look from one to the other, but they don't reply. Fighting to keep a smile of bemusement from giving him away, Vaughn folds his arms and plants his feet as he scrutinizes the two guilty parties looking at me.

"Well?" I prod. Still no reply. They have to explain or I won't stop asking. I just need to keep silent a few moments longer because guilty parties inevitably dislike long and uncomfortable silences.

Vaughn ends the suspense by demanding, "Are you two fucking?"

"Vaughn!" I snap in exasperation. He's a good man in a fight, but the fine points of interrogation sadly elude him.

"What did you just say?" Aimes growls back. "Do you think she's a common whore?"

"I didn't fail to notice you didn't answer my question," I reply.

"Nor mine," Vaughn adds.

I hold up my hand at Vaughn. "Don't answer his question." With my best commanding stare at Ember, I say, "But I'd like to know how it is that earlier your clothes were dirty from the trail and now they're sparkling clean and yet we've not come across any mode of water?"

"And even if we had," Vaughn adds. "And you had washed your clothing, it would never have dried in such a short amount of time."

I nod. "Are you employing some sort of witchcraft?"

To her credit, Ember's face turns to stone at my question. I have a feeling that if this were a palace interrogation, nothing short of the rack could make her talk.

"I've been helping to… to clean her," Aimes finally replies.

"With what? Your tongue?" Vaughn grunts.

"Vaughn," I grumble, shaking my head. "Have you no couth at all?"

My gruff man-at-arms shrugs. "I'll give you an answer if you tell me what 'couth' means."

I rub the bridge of my nose. "Never mind." As he shrugs, I look towards Aimes. "How are you doing it?"

Aimes hesitates for a moment or two and then looks at Ember, who's already looking at him.

"Aimes," she starts. "You don't have to—"

He shakes his head and looks back at me. "Magic," he says. "Or witchcraft, if you prefer."

At my and Vaughn's obvious shocked reaction, Aimes carefully explains his unique mystical talent and how he discovered it. Everything makes perfect sense now. Still, I'm surprised he'd expose such a secret to a relative stranger like Ember. Her obvious physical perfection aside, she must have another quality that convinced him to trust her with his secret. I can only imagine that 'other quality' exists between her legs.

"Well, that explains that," I finish, turning back to my meager snack. "Let's finish supper. We've got a long way to go before nightfall."

By the time the sun dips below the horizon, we veer away from the river, heading into less traveled territory. In the small clearing where we tuck ourselves, there are sharp thorn bushes and not much else.

"Since we're too far from the river for bathing," I advise Aimes, "you'll probably have to hack through these bushes to blaze a path for Ember." I try hard not to sound bitter when I mention his blooming friendship with her. But I'm not fooling anyone.

"Oh, no need for that," Ember says as she casually reaches out to Aimes and pulls up her long sleeve to reveal her alabaster skin underneath. As she does so, I barely detect the faintest ripples of something under the surface. No human woman has skin like that. What exactly is she?

"You aren't just human," Vaughn says, apparently noticing her skin as well.

A bit of self-consciousness creeps into her face. "I'm... different... probably weird." I can tell she's uncomfortable with her announcement and she immediately turns her attention to Aimes, who focuses on cleaning her by touching her (as far as I can tell). Then he moves to cleaning the grime and dust off her clothing, again by simply touching it.

"That's not the word I would choose," he says in a voice that's almost a whisper, but I'm still able to make out the words. "I find you exquisite."

Then the man's completely taken with her, is he? Glancing up from her newly cleaned clothes, I catch Aimes' gaze and lift a single eyebrow in question. He breathes in deeply, then shrugs. I suppose I can hardly blame him for stating the obvious. Well, to everyone except Ember herself. She doesn't have a clue what classic beauty she possesses.

Vaughn and I watch Aimes as he takes her hands and focuses on her. It's a gradual transition that begins with her hair. The pale blonde locks pop free of their braids before bouncing into silvery waves that fall across her perfect form. Immediately, my attention shifts to the mounds of her breasts that pop out of the top of her corseted dress.

I turn away. I doubt she'd appreciate the clear evidence of my arousal. Usually, I would go hunting in a situation like this one—just to get my mind off it—but it's too late now for that. We'll have to ration the last of the jerky. We must reach Ascor tomorrow or we'll wind up grazing like our horses. Getting the jerky from our packs distracts me from the previous scene and I stow it in the back of my mind. That's where it needs to stay.

When I glance at Vaughn, I notice he hasn't pulled his eyes away from Ember. It's become quite obvious that Vaughn and I are more than interested in bedding this woman, but Aimes got to her first. And you don't take a friend's woman for your own.

By the time I return with the jerky, Ember is busily spreading her tent out on the ground and Aimes joins her on top of it. As they look up at the stars, he points out the different constellations in the sky, making her smile. If only such a face would look my way...

After allotting them their share of the jerky, I walk over to Vaughn to give him his. I recognize the same mournful regret in his eyes.

"I'll be glad when we get to Ascor," he says before taking a bite.

"You and me both."

Nothing more needs to be said. We just sit quietly and eat, both of us watching Ember and Aimes from a distance. This magical ability of his must be the answer to their sudden friendship, I assume. It's not, as Vaughn thought—that they were fucking. It's simply that Aimes has somehow won her trust with the small acts of kindness he's shown her.

Soon, I'm lying in a rough bed of a blanket and my rolled-up outer coat as I stare up at the night sky. I eat the last of my jerky before finally drifting off to sleep.

We reach Ascor by the early afternoon.

We're all famished and dusty from the trail and though we're happy to have arrived, our eager entrance into town is eclipsed by a procession of Princess Carmine's guard. Surprisingly, the princess herself comes into view as they march. We all watch, mesmerized by the rare sight. Once they pass, we continue on. A decent meal would be nice, but first things first. At my insistence, we head to The Wicked Lyre.

One look at the pitted stone building and its rotting wooden shutters makes Vaughn grunt. "This place is desolate. No one's been here for a very long time. Are you sure this is the place?"

"I am," Ember replies, her flat tone telling him she doesn't appreciate any doubts regarding her skill.

Vaughn approaches the boarded-up front door of the tavern, examining it. "Well, let's get going then."

"Wait," I reply, nervously eyeing the street. "The last thing we want is to attract attention. Perhaps there's a back door that's not quite so noticeable to passersby."

Vaughn nods and grunts his concurrence. Meanwhile, we make our way around the building. Pulling the boards off the back door, Vaughn tosses them to the side. The chained door behind the boards is partially rotten. With a big grin, he kicks it in and his big boot splits the door in two, sending sections of wood to either side.

"Merciful goddess, could you be less subtle?" Aimes admonishes him.

Holding up a hand, I look down the lane to see if our commotion was observed. When a few moments pass, I wave us toward the now-open door.

Once we enter, I let my eyes adjust to the scarcity of light. "Look everywhere and under everything."

Ember seems forlorn as she investigates the bar. Shattered glass and piles of dirt cover the floor. I can only assume many a squatter and/or vandal came here before the place was sealed shut. It's a mess and Ember is the last person who should be witnessing it, given her issues with places like this.

"Ember, you can wait outside until we're finished," I offer.

She gives me a grateful smile when Vaughn busts open another window to let in more light. Suddenly, everything goes straight to the nine hells. Five men with heavy beards appear from the rooms at the side of our entrance. The robes they wear indicate they're Hassan's men. One grabs Ember while the remaining four attack us with drawn knives. We're too close to use our swords, so we lurch for the debris on the floor in order to retaliate. We're quickly embroiled in the first all-out brawl this tavern has seen since it was officially closed.

Ember screams when her abductor tries to drag her through the back door. I manage to knock out my attacker by smashing a chair over his head. Before I can reach her, another man grabs me by the shoulder and throws me against the bar. I feel something crack before pain shoots through me and I punch him in the throat. Sliding down the bar, I have to struggle to remain on my feet. I stagger backwards near Ember's captor.

I'm hurt and from the way I'm losing stamina and strength quickly, I'm fairly sure I'm hurt badly. Regardless, my only concern is for Ember, something which shocks me, but I don't have time to further ponder it.

Instead, I notice the bastard has her delicate wrist in one hand while with the other he wields a curved knife. He turns the knife my way just as I manage to use whatever strength I have left as I lunge for him, slapping the knife free from his grasp. At the same moment, Ember reaches down to the floor and grabs a shard of glass. It's akin to slow motion as I watch her stand up and, with no expression on her face, she simply jabs the shard into his neck. Then she backs away as he releases her and there's shock in her expression. Clearly, she's never killed a man before.

The bastard screams, but it's a garbled sound. He reaches up to grasp his throat in order to staunch the blood now gushing out, but that will do little to stop his life from fleeing his body. It was a killing blow Ember gave him. Staggering backward, he falls to the floor at her feet, his eyes wide and in death's grasp.

Aimes, meanwhile, blocks the door in his brawl with another attacker. Aimes is a skilled fighter and I'm not concerned with him. Instead, I summon up my rapidly waning energy and limp towards Ember as I escort her to the broken window.

"You're hurt," she whispers.

"My only concern is getting you away from these sons of bitches," I answer, wincing as I do so. I don't intend to seem like a baby, but the pain is fairly intense. I push what remaining shards of glass still decorate the window and then cup my hands as I lean down. Ember seems to understand and puts her foot in my impromptu stirrup as I stand up and lift her up and out of the window.

She jumps from the window and at that moment, stars begin to swim in my vision and I fall against the wall. I'm not sure if Ember has made it safely to the ground below, but at this point, I can barely stay conscious. Steeling myself with a deep breath, I turn around and spot the final attacker attempting to strike Vaughn from behind. I totter toward him, but the pain from whatever that bastard did to me isn't subsiding.

I fear I'm blacking out.

CHAPTER NINE
EMBER

I'm concerned that Blake could be hurt badly—so much so, that I don't immediately look down after he helps me out the window. The ground is much further than it appears. Worse yet, it's on an incline. Thus, I find myself suddenly flying face first into the jagged rocks at the bottom of the hillside.

This is it. I'm going to die a horrible death behind some gods-forsaken pub.

I scream, preparing for the pain that's about to engulf me. My hands shoot out, as if they could stop the inevitable from coming. But, just as I'm about to collide with the rocky terrain, I'm suddenly lifted high, up and away from the rocks as if a might wind simply surged beneath me.

It takes me a second to realize I'm not simply imagining what's happening, but as my feet touch the ground, strong hands secure my waist and steady me. Yet, when I look down at myself, there are no hands at all. In fact, I'm standing alone. Catching my breath, I find myself standing on a staircase that wasn't there a minute ago.

Hearing someone behind me, I turn to watch Aimes as he approaches me and grabs me around the waist, slinging me over his shoulder like a sack of wheat.

"What are you doing?" I ask, fear and shock and disbelief all taking turns stabbing my brain. I just can't understand what just happened and how it was possible and who was responsible.

"Getting us away from here," he replies, running around the side of the pub and onto the road. The speed with which he moves doesn't seem… natural, and I have to wonder if it's yet another manifestation of this incredible magic he possesses.

Looking back, Vaughn and Blake are right on our heels. Well, Vaughn is on our heels and doing his best to act the part of crutch to Blake, who's covered in blood and limping badly. His usually olive coloring is as white as a ghost.

Chasing them, one of the men demands we stop. A small glass wall shoots up behind us, and the man smashes into it with comical clumsiness. The streets below our feet then begin to transform, becoming pure glass as Aimes sets me down. Soon, all of us are sliding down a slick embankment. Thankfully, only a grassy knoll lies at the bottom.

The moment we hit the grass, we stand up and run. A loud caw fills our ears from the sky above. I look up to see a man riding a Roc. I've never seen a real one of these immense birds before, but the long thin beak and razor sharp claws match all the pictures I've studied. Their size—more dragon than bird—makes them even more terrifying.

"Head for the trees," Vaughn shouts, pulling my arm. Though I'm fully aware of the danger, I can't resist the urge to observe this magnificent predator of the sky. It really is a majestic animal, so deadly but so beautiful a creation. I start running again, noting with some pride that I'm keeping up with the men. Fairly soon, Vaughn has to grip Blake and heft him over his shoulders. Quite a feat but Vaughn is an enormous man. Large and solidly muscled. Even with the added weight, he manages to keep up with us.

The dense trees eventually open up to a broad clearing and we continue to run. I wonder if we weren't safer inside the grove. Either way, we're utterly at the mercy of our pursuer.

The Roc lands less than three feet from us, and we're forced to stop. The man atop it says, "Stop or I'll unleash this beast on the lot of you, even the woman." For emphasis, the bird stretches its great wings, sealing off any means of escape. There's no way out.

Apparently satisfied that we'll cooperate, the man jumps down from his mount, walking over to us with a weary look. He holds out a hand.

"Give me the map."

"What map?" Aimes asks.

"Don't play coy," the man grumbles. "I saw you with it in the tavern. Why do you think my men and I were there in the first place?"

"I thought you grew out of the filth on the ground, like Cadmus's teeth," Vaughn growls.

"Droll," the man says without amusement. He gestures with his hand again. "Now... the map."

"If you're referring to the map that's *supposed to be* in the tavern, we don't have it," Blake explains, and his voice even sounds pained. "We were looking for it when your men jumped us."

"Do you take me for a fool?" the man asks, his patience clearly rapidly dwindling. "We scoured every inch of that tavern before you arrived. Thus, the map you have must be the one we seek."

Aimes looks at him incredulously. "And why exactly would we return to the tavern if we already had the map in our possession?"

The man's brow furrows. "This Roc will rip you all apart, at my order. And I have no qualms peeling the map off the bones of whatever is left of you after his hearty repast."

Despite the great bird standing before us, Vaughn takes a defiant step forward. "I'd sooner die than hand your master, Hassan, anything."

"Hassan? My master?" the man scowls. "Don't be daft. I need the map in order to *stop* Hassan."

"What?" Blake inquires, glancing at the others in confusion.

The man sighs. "Perhaps we both have false impressions of each other." He adds, "Hassan is holding my clan captive. I need the Blue Faerie's wand—the whereabouts of which the map details— because that's the only way I can save them."

Vaughn considers this. "That sounds like a terrible problem, but a personal one."

"As of this moment, *your* problem is also *my* problem."

"Really?" Vaughn asks with a sneer. "Last I checked, there are three of us and one of you."

"Actually, there are *four* of you," the man corrects him. "One is hurt badly, and the dainty lass can't fight." He points to his flying pet. "And don't forget the Roc, who has a nasty temper and hasn't eaten yet today."

"We don't care," Aimes replies, edging his way forward.

"So you refuse?"

"That's a fair assumption," Blake replies.

"So it is," the man says, turning back to the Roc and waving his hand upward. The bird begins flapping its great wings, blotting out the sun above us with its sheer size. It hovers, its steely eyes pinning us to the ground.

I know I must do something, or this will end in disaster. "Wait!"

The man turns around, seemingly surprised that I can speak at all. Aimes, Vaughn and Blake share his surprise. All three of them look at me as though I've grown a third eye. Granted, it's unlike me to speak up, but the thought of being eaten by a Roc is even less appealing than finding my courage.

"We all seek the same thing," I tell the man. "So, perhaps instead of fighting, we should unite forces."

The man's laughter is lyrical if it weren't so mocking. "And why, in the name of all that's holy, would I do that? I've already proven to be more than your equal in brawn. I certainly don't need a fragile lass who could shatter at the slightest touch."

"Someone who has ridden as far as I have in the last week is anything but delicate," I argue, brandishing my indignation like a weapon. "Besides, I can decipher the map faster than anyone. And time is of the essence for all of us."

He purses his lips and nods. "There is some truth to that, yes, but what's to stop me from killing your friends and forcing you to decipher the clues for me alone?"

"Good luck with that," Vaughn chuckles. "Stubborn as a tick on the hide of a horse, that one is," he says and motions to me with his chin. "She'd sooner let that bird feast on her for breakfast than be forced to help anyone she doesn't want to." I sense the pride and respect in his words.

While I'm a bit surprised by his sentiment, I don't respond. Turning my attention back to the man in front of us, I watch him stroke his chin in contemplation before waving his hand downward. The Roc lands on his right before hopping over to stand behind him once again.

"Very well," he says finally. "I agree to a temporary alliance." As he speaks, he doesn't take his eyes off me, as if he doesn't trust me—even more so than my fellow travelers.

"Good," I say. "May we ask your name?"

"Sinbad."

"That's it? Just Sinbad?"

"Just Sinbad," he says with a wave and a winning smile. "And now that you know my name, I would like to know yours."

Despite the previous tension, I smile. "Ember." I gesture to my traveling companions one by one. "Aimes, Vaughn, and Blake." I purposely omit Blake's title because I'm not sure if being the prince of Sweetland will help or hinder him in this instance. Better not to risk it.

"Unpleasant circumstances aside, gentlemen," Sinbad says with a bow, "it is a pleasure to make your acquaintance."

"Likewise," Blake replies, considerably less than charmed. "Now, can we get back to the question of finding the map?"

"You truly don't have it?" Sinbad groans.

"We already told you we didn't," Aimes growls with impatience.

Sinbad rubs the side of his head. "Fine. Let us return to the tavern to look again." He sighs and adds, "Assuming it's still there."

"It's not still there," Vaughn says before pulling a parchment free of his jacket and holding it up.

"And when were you going to tell us you found it?" Aimes asks with audible annoyance.

Vaughn shrugs. "I'm telling you now, aren't I?"

I frown at him. "We got attacked before we could even look for it."

"I grabbed it right after you and Aimes fell down the hillside," he explains. "It was hanging on the wall behind a painting Aimes knocked loose when he went after you. I snatched it when I ran for the door."

Blake looks at him with annoyance.

"What?" Vaughn exclaims. "When did I have time to tell you before now?"

"True," Blake concedes. "Now that we've got it, we'd best take a look at it."

"Not here, my new friend," Sinbad corrects him. "Hassan's men will waste little time pursuing us and you... are quickly losing your life's blood."

"Is it so bad?" Aimes asks as he turns to look at Blake.

"Then where do we review the map?" Blake asks, ignoring the expressions of concern on all our faces.

Even though I've hated Blake up until this point, I can honestly say I don't hate him any longer. Not after he risked his life for me. And, I also have to admit to myself, that though I don't agree with the way in which he recruited me, his quest is a good one. A noble one. So, no, I don't consider Blake, Vaughn or Aimes my enemies any longer. In fact, it seems they are quickly becoming my friends.

Sinbad pushes both his hands downward. The Roc goes as flat as his large body will allow. "I know the perfect place. If you will all climb aboard...?"

CHAPTER TEN
EMBER

I'm flying!

I've been up in the air for several minutes and I still can't get over that fact. Despite having to hang on for dear life, my excitement is brimming. The chance to experience this—on the back of a Roc, to boot—almost makes this expedition worth all the aggravation I've suffered.

Speaking of, I look over at Vaughn, who is clinging to the bird with one hand and Blake with the other. Blake leans against him and still has a pained expression on his face.

"How bad is it?" I ask Vaughn.

He shakes his head. "Not too bad or he wouldn't have lasted this long."

"I'm fine," Blake nearly interrupts. "And I'd appreciate it if you two would stop fussing over me."

"You're not fine," I say as I point at his shirt. "For one, you're covered in blood."

He grins at me. "And how do you know that blood is mine?"

I shake my head as I sigh out a long and exasperated breath and figure Vaughn is right—Blake is hurt, yes, but his wounds must not be life-threatening. Besides, there's nothing any of us can do at the moment when we're clinging to the bird's feathers for deal life.

Speaking of, we soar over the trees that embody the Forest of No Return. Sinbad's huge bird banks in that direction and we fly around the edge until we finally land in a dark valley. Perhaps once the valley was beautiful. Now it's black and charred. A ruined landscape. Improbably, there's a cottage nearby, appearing untouched by this place's horrors.

"This seems too open," Blake remarks as we dismount the Roc.

"This deep into such an inhospitable territory?" Sinbad replies amusedly. "We would scarcely be safer if we were in the deepest cave." He pulls out a piece of fruit—a pomegranate—and throws it towards the Roc's gigantic beak. As the great bird swallows the treat in one gulp, he says, "You four take the cottage. We'll rest out here."

"All of us can fit in the cabin," I say as the Roc squawks a loud protest. "All right, maybe not you."

Sinbad chuckles. "Very kind of you to think of me, but any true sailor prefers to sleep beneath the stars. Besides, I feel trapped indoors."

"It's going to be a cold night," Aimes says, and I appreciate the fact that he cares for Sinbad's well-being, just as I do. Aimes is a caring person, in general, and I must admit, I'm happy I've met him.

Sinbad strokes his bird's enormous wing. "Indeed, which is why this great beast shall be my blanket when I lie down."

"One thing I haven't figured out," Vaughn says, raising his index finger. "How did you know about the map in the tavern?"

"Not all of Hassan's underlings are as competent as the bravos you fought," Sinbad explains. "One of them told me about the map and said Hassan intended to turn the spoils over to Morningstar. I planned to steal the map from whomever came out of the tavern when you turned up."

"So you were already overhead when we arrived?" I ask.

"If you'd bothered to look up, you would have seen us soaring through the sky, watching you enter."

"Well, good thing to note for the next time we're invading a tavern searching for a legendary map," Vaughn grunts.

Sinbad hums. "Since I shall remain outside, I volunteer to take first watch."

"I don't think so," Vaughn says, his eyes narrowing in suspicion. "You might be a friend; but you also might not be. Until I know for sure, we'll take care of our own."

"Which means, keep a watchful eye on me," Sinbad observes.

Vaughn grins. "Good to know we understand one another."

"Direct speech is like a desert oasis, rare but bracing," Sinbad says, returning Vaughn's grin. "We both know where we stand."

"We could do with some food and we still have to care for Blake and his wounds," I say, not meaning to change the subject, but there are more important things on which we should be focused.

"I'm fine," Blake barks out again but I ignore him, instead watching as Sinbad reaches into his pack on the Roc and thrusts a bag of fruit before us. The smell and shape confirms the fruit is pomegranates. All of us are famished and promptly devour the offered nourishment.

The Roc gives another annoyed squawk, prompting Sinbad to say, "Oh, hush, you overgrown buzzard. You've been fed and they haven't."

After making short work of the fruit, Vaughn says, "I'll take first watch while everyone gets some sleep." He looks at Aimes. "Second watch at midnight?"

"Agreed," Aimes replies, already at the edge of the open cottage door. "God and goddess, but I'm exhausted."

"Don't forget, we need to dress Blake's wounds."

"I can bloody well dress them myself!" Blake responds.

Aimes looks at me. "His hardheadedness may someday cost him his life."

###

Even though he doesn't want me to help, I assist Blake with building a fire in the cottage chimney. He's doing his best to be stoic, but it's obvious he's in pain. Finally, I can't stand it anymore and say, "You're injured and even though you're doing your best to act the part of unharmed, it's not working."

"I'm fine," he grumbles. "And I can see to my wounds myself."

"Stubborn, yes, but fine no."

He glances at the now-snoring Aimes, who fills the cottage with sonorous sounds. After Blake repeatedly refused either of us to 'fuss' over him, as he termed it, Aimes gave up and fell asleep on one of the beds.

"If that wound isn't treated, it will get infected, grow rancid, and you'll most likely die," I say.

He glances at Aimes again. "I can wait until he wakes up."

I jab a spot where the blood is still flowing, which makes him flinch. "That wound says otherwise."

He reluctantly nods and tries to strip off his outer layers, but doing so is too painful for him, so I manage the duties for him instead. Once I get his shirt off, I can finally get a closer look at the wound.

"It's bad," I mutter as I kneel and inspect it.

"How bad," he groans.

"It looks like someone took a broken bottle to you," I reply, shaking my head. "There's still a piece of glass stuck in the middle of a very deep gash."

"Well, that explains the cracking noise I heard," he sighs. "Better than seeing one of my bones sticking out."

"True... let me get something to treat it."

In the kitchen, I manage to dig up some rags and a bottle of cheap corn liquor. I return to the fire and use one of the rags to grasp the glass shard.

"This is going to hurt," I warn him.

He nods. "Do it."

With a firm grip on the glass, I begin wiggling it loose. Every jiggle from loosening the embedded shard makes him audibly suck in another pain-filled breath. When I finally pull the shard free, blood pours out like a fountain. I staunch the blood flow with more rags, pressing them tightly until the blood stops penetrating them. Blake braces himself with the side of the chimney, doing his best to hold still. Once the bleeding stops, I pour alcohol over the wound to cleanse it. He moans loudly, gritting his teeth while I tie the last few rags around his waist and form a makeshift bandage. Not the best healing method in Fantasia, but it'll have to do for now.

"Try not to sleep on that side," I tell him. "I'll check the wound again in the morning."

When he looks at me, I notice the sweat pouring off his brow and instantly recall the blood that was pouring out of his side.

"Thanks. Mind if I have the rest of that bottle?" he asks.

I hand it to him. "It might—"

He takes a healthy slug from the bottle and moments later, drains it dry. How silly of me to think he intended to use the gut rot on his wound! He drops the bottle at his side and I bemoan the loss. Alcohol isn't my first choice of cleaning agent, but it does in a pinch and I was planning on using it to clean myself once I'd seen to Blake's wounds. Of course, I could ask Aimes and I'm sure he'd oblige me happily, but I don't want to wake him up. He needs his sleep. But, I'm really feeling unclean without so much as a drop of water in this remote cottage or a nearby creek outside.

Doing my best to ignore my state of uncleanliness temporarily, I say, "I'm sorry you got hurt trying to help me."

"You owe me no apology, Ember," Blake assures me. "Any of us would have done the same. The last thing we want is to see you hurt."

Were I calmer—and cleaner—I'd point out his blatant contradiction: he already threatened the well-being of my family. But, I don't say anything because I figure he did what he had to do in order to cajole me into this trip. I never would have agreed to go unless he'd taken the measures he did and he must have bet on that.

And, don't forget, this trip is a noble one, I remind myself. *It's not as though Blake's trying to benefit himself. He's trying to save Fantasia.*

Yes, Blake is… dare I admit it? A good man.

And I can't help but think about the fact that he's gotten hurt trying to rescue me. That thought leads to other thoughts—namely how useless I am. "You must think I'm so neurotic, so... hopeless." I spit the last word out like it's a familial curse.

Blake extends a gentle finger to caress my cheek. "You're far from hopeless. In fact, that big, beautiful brain of yours is the only reason we knew where to go at all." He cups my lower jaw. "If anything, I'm in awe of you. You're the cleverest woman I've ever met... and…" His voice trails.

"And?" I ask, even though I'm surprised by my own question because ordinarily I'd avoid such emotional conversations as this one like the plague.

"You're the most beautiful, too."

I look up to find him smiling softly at me. I can't fathom what he's just said—he thinks I'm the most beautiful woman he's ever seen? Him—a prince? And one with quite the colorful reputation. With the firelight flickering across his face, he looks even more handsome than the first time I saw him in the rock garden.

"Thank you," I whisper and find I can't break his gaze, just as it seems he can't break mine.

"You and Aimes," he starts.

I shake my head. "We are friends," I answer, even as the truth burns deep inside me—yes, Aimes and I are just friends, but that's not to say I don't have feelings for him—feelings that extend beyond the realm of friendship. Of course, Aimes hasn't confessed to feeling anything for me, so maybe that's why I take comfort in my admission that we aren't anything more.

I watch Blake, feeling as if I'm in slow motion, as his eyelids grow heavier and he leans closer to me. Fairly soon, his lips are on mine and I don't stop him from kissing me. His lips are soft and full, so warm and inviting. My skin heats up from fire that suddenly burns inside me and our kiss deepens.

Even as I don't fully understand what's happening, can't grasp it entirely, I watch Blake as he pulls away from me and then my attention is drawn to his naked chest. A naked chest I was treating only moments ago.

His body is muscular and his shoulders are broad, narrowing into a smaller waist and very long legs. It's obvious he has royal blood. His skin is smooth and toned, appropriate to someone of his bearing. I wonder how many women have been lucky enough to see him like this. While men like Aimes and Vaughn carry the scars of their battles, Blake possesses no such blemishes. So far as I can see, the wound I just cleaned will leave the only scar he'll ever have.

And that's when I remember why I'm here—that this man has forced me into this position by using my family as leverage against me. Even if I've mostly forgiven him, I still hold on to that shred of a reason to keep distance between us. Even though the reason is mostly extinct now, owing to the new spin I have on things, it doesn't change the fact that I don't want to get involved with him or any of them. I can't get involved. I'm just… not wired that way. No, instead, I'm timid and afraid of everything and everyone.

And yet… is that really true?

After everything I've seen on this trip thus far, all the experiences I've had and the things I've done, like killing a man, for example… I'm not the same person I was. So, no, I'm not timid and afraid any longer.

I pull away from him and back away a few steps.

"I… I need to get to bed," I say.

CHAPTER ELEVEN
VAUGHN

Stepping into the cottage to awaken Aimes, I spot Blake and Ember kissing by the fire. Clearly, Blake must have recovered from his wounds. Or recovered enough, anyway. Not wanting to play the part of third wheel, I immediately retreat outside as I try to calm the sporadic beating of my heart.

Son of a bitch! Am I the only one who hasn't sampled her? I'm fairly sure Aimes has had his turn with her and now Blake? Granted, I'm not as handsome as those two, but I can easily hold my own with women, who usually fall for my physical brawn. It's not as though I'm an unattractive man, but there's nothing soft or feminine about me. Perhaps that's what Ember's drawn to?

Yet, Ember is unlike any other woman I've known. In my experience, women fall into one of two categories, either they're kept or they're fearless. The kept ones are docile, doing anything to appease the hand that feeds them. The fearless ones do as they please with whomever pleases them. Ember's an enigma because she displays a bit of both. Sometimes, she's subdued and seeks someone to care for her. Other times, she's bold, not holding her anger back. I find her not only bewildering but also captivating.

But, the puzzle of Ember must be temporarily postponed because we have more important things on which to focus. Stealing my reserve, I march back into the house and this time, I find Blake and Ember separated, each on their own bed. Thank the gods.

Walking to Aimes, I shake him awake. He groans and tries to roll over and go back to sleep, so I pat him on the shoulder a couple of times to ensure he's coherent. He gives me a wan smile and, getting up, grabs his gear.

I find my attention again returns to Ember, where she's nestled on her side and appears to be asleep, her eyes closed. Then my attention returns to Blake as I wonder if the kiss was the extent of their tryst. I can't help but hope so. And that realization bothers me because I shouldn't give a damn about what Ember does with her body. Yet, I do.

Regardless, neither Aimes nor I can compete with a prince. Doesn't matter how many women we've bedded. If a prince enters the game, we don't warrant a second glance. It's no big deal, really, just the way things are. Knowing that, I still feel a little jealous about Blake's luck of birthright. Because that's really all it is—the luck of the draw.

That aside, I strip off some of my gear and prepare for sleep. Sitting down on the edge of the bed Aimes just crawled out of, I can't wait to close my eyes and drift into the wonderful world of sleep.

"It's a good bed," Aimes mutters, grabbing my attention as he pulls on his left boot. "There's a spirit about it."

"A spirit?" I repeat doubtfully, frowning. Yes, Aimes is my friend, but that doesn't mean he isn't a bit odd sometimes. "As in, it's haunted?"

"No, not exactly, but someone named Reve likes to linger near the pillows."

I stare at him for a bit before shrugging his statement off. "I'm too damn tired to care about ghosts. Time for some shut-eye."

"Sweet dreams," he says, slipping on his other boot and heading out the door without casting a second glance at Ember or Blake. Perhaps one look was enough. Maybe I'm not the only one experiencing some jealousy over the fair, young Ms. Limus.

I awaken shortly after dawn, hearing voices talking quietly. Sitting up, I stretch, walking barefoot to the table where those damned pomegranates occupy most of the space. Beside them is the map I retrieved from the tavern—the one everyone appears to be after.

Sinbad silently offers me one of his numerous fruits and I dig in, staining my fingers with the purple-red juice. Aimes must have used his cleaning magic on Ember, judging by her glowing skin and spotless clothes. Her hair flows in long waves down her back as she opens the map. I feel a stir in my loins and have to consciously ignore it. The sooner we finish our business and return Ember to her life, the better.

But, back to the map. In only moments, she deciphers the code. Blake quickly produces an inkpot and quill so she can mark which direction we need to go. Sinbad is visibly impressed, almost as much as I. Of course, I can see it's more than just her map-reading skills that he appreciates. I nearly choke on my rage and frustration at the idea that even he might have a better chance with her than I do.

I mutter a brief apology as I get up from the table to step outside. The Roc is resting on the ground, looking like a cat poised to pounce on any mouse foolhardy enough to cross its territory. I may be angry at my own jealousy, but I'm not suicidal, and I give the monstrous bird wide berth. The path is slightly buried under the ashes of the fires that have raged through this area, destroying near everything in sight.

It's not long before I hear the sound of water flowing nearby.

It can't be, I think before following the gurgling until, lo and behold, I arrive at a clear blue stream. Watching the sky for any overhead threats—the Roc being the least of my worries—I fill my canteen with cool, fresh drinking water. Taking a swig, I have to marvel how something so pristine as this creek manages to survive in such desolate territory. How askew things are right now. The looming battle is on the horizon, so the usual rules no longer apply. Anything can and will happen. Anything, that is, except what I want the most right now.

Staring at the refreshing stream, I think about Ember's glorious face and I wonder if she'd be even more glorious emerging from the river, dripping wet, the water beading on her nipples and navel. I can imagine her hair slicked back against her head, her womanhood dewy with glistening droplets. Now I'm getting hard. I caution myself to calm down. No good getting all hot for someone who has no interest in me.

Soon enough, I'll have to part ways with her, anyway. Once we find the wand, I'll be off to the Guild. They have to mobilize every man they can find to disseminate all the stones Carmine stole. We have to locate the rest of the Chosen ones too, before time runs out. If the witches in Fantasia have it right, we've only a month or two before the seals break. Seals that keep Morningstar imprisoned.

Pulling one of those stones from my pocket, I press it and feel its shape in my hand. To my surprise, it begins glowing red. I'm certain my gasp is loud, but I can't help it. The color vibrating through the cracks in the stone is mesmerizing. Furthermore, I've never seen the stone light up like this.

That's when I hear something from behind me. The sounds of footfalls. My attention turns to whoever is approaching, cracking twigs underfoot. I'm about to put the stone away when Ember emerges from the bushes that grow nearest the water.

"Shouldn't you be with Blake planning our next move?" I ask with some discomfort.

"Already have," she replies. "He wanted to fetch you, but I volunteered. I was worried you..."

Her simple words captivate me in a way the stone can't match. Then she notices the stone and asks, "What is that?" while pointing towards my hand.

I'm astounded when the stone's red glow increases more brightly with each step she takes toward me. The closer she comes, the deeper and brighter the red glow. How can that be? Unless…

"It's one of princess Carmine's stones," I answer as I approach her and, noticing the crimson deepening, I hold the stone out to her. The light it emits is now almost blinding. She reaches out and takes it in her hand, to examine it closer. It pulses a fiery red, as if coming alive in her dainty hands.

And that's when I realize what this means.

"Vaughn, why does it seem like the stone is growing brighter the longer I hold it?" Ember asks me, still visibly confused.

"Don't you see?" I reply with a grin, shaking my head at her ignorance. How can she not know?! "The glowing of the stone can only mean one thing... you're a Chosen One!"

CHAPTER TWELVE
EMBER

Vaughn's words echo in my head hours later as we ride on the back of Sinbad's Roc. Naturally, I deny his claim. How could I, of all people, be one of the Chosen? The only thing I can do well is clean and decipher codes and that's what I continue to respond every time one of them argues that I am Chosen. Vaughn's incessant answer is that the stone can't lie.

Blake, Aimes and Sinbad agree with him. In fact, I'm surprised by how quickly they accept the completely absurd idea that I'm among this noble group. They're fully convinced before I've ever even given the thought the benefit of possibility.

But even then, there is no way it can be true. I'm just… I'm so damned weak and too broken to be one of the famed Chosen. The only skill I have is my deductive mind, hardly enough to use in battle or contend with the prophecy the Chosen Ones foresee. If the seals break as soon as the witches predict, I can't imagine how to prepare for the carnage that will unfold. No matter what Vaughn thinks, I'm convinced the stone must be wrong.

"Anoka Desert is dead ahead," Blake calls out from behind me, being careful not to disrupt the bandage from around his middle. "Is everyone ready?"

Speaking of all the things I'm unprepared for... I think to myself.

The Anoka Desert is not a place most people would dare set foot in. It's barren, dry, and massive. It takes miles to traverse and offers no source of hydration, thus you must carry in your own water. But thirst isn't the only way to die in the unforgiving desert. There are sand beasts that prey on anything that moves, and dust storms that are so blinding with whirling sand that you lose all sense of direction. Camels can't even cross it, never mind the horses we left behind.

What a stroke of rare good luck when we joined up with Sinbad! His Roc soars above the sandy terrain below while we balance securely on its back. The Roc's able to fly above the threats we'd otherwise face below. Not to mention with the bird's incredible speed, he's saving us days, or possibly weeks, of traveling time. Yes, we are quite fortuitous indeed!

The pervasive sand floats up on the wind, covering us because we aren't very far above the ground. We need to fly low in order to follow the map. Sadly, it's very difficult to distract myself from the dust and sand that splatters me during the flight.

The only serenity I find in this sand-filled hell comes from Vaughn, himself. He holds me tightly in his powerful arms, and I feel safe—as if with his arms around me, there's no way I can fall off my perch. Meanwhile, he plays mental games with me to keep me occupied. He tells me to recite all the facts I know regarding everything from dragons to Blake's lineage. So that's what I do—prattle on and on and on about this and that, spouting facts I'm sure everyone is tired of listening to. Yet, all of them remain quiet except for the moments when whatever I'm talking about seems to strike a chord of interest and they ask a question here or there. Otherwise, they just simply listen.

My nerves are slowly settling. Whenever I tire of my recitations, Vaughn switches the subject to arithmetic, giving me long equations to solve. This technique keeps me calm—mostly—but fears of inadequacy still haunt me. Every girl dreams of being a princess, but no sane girl would want to become a Chosen One.

"There's the oasis!" Blake calls, pointing to the heart-shaped watering hole when we fly over it. Despite its name, it's not a good place from which to drink, as the water is poisoned by parasites. One sip from the spring will kill anyone who dares to drink it.

"Very good, Blake," Sinbad calls out from the front. "As I recall, we need to go fifty miles further to the right and look for a large stone."

"Not just any stone," Aimes adds. "A *blood-red* stone. It might look black from the sky."

"I see it!" I shout, pointing to a rock that suddenly appears in the same direction in which we're flying. After a few minutes, Sinbad banks to right before coaxing the Roc to land beside the stone. Once the colossal bird alights, we all jump off. I try to ignore the sand seeping into my shoes as my feet sink into the hot grains.

Blake walks around the base of the smooth crimson rock, taking sips from his canteen. "So, what do we do now?"

I frown and try to recall what the map said. "Per the last cipher, the line on the rock will show us the way." But, there are no openings or footholds on the rock, none that I can see anyway, so something doesn't seem right.

"What line?" Vaughn asks. "Only lines I see are the shadows the rock is casting."

I pull open the map to review it. When I reread the notation, everything clicks into place. "I forgot the actual words," I say. "The line of the *sun* will show us the way."

"Oh, that clears everything up," Vaughn sneers sarcastically.

Disregarding his bad temper, I look closer at the drawing under the notation. It plainly shows a sun directly above the rock and the shadow pointing straight down. I check my pocket watch—still working despite the travails I've been through—and I see it's nearly noon. "If we wait three more minutes," I say, "we should have our answer."

Sinbad spreads his hands out wide and the Roc obeys by opening his large wings to provide shadow and cool us from the sun's incessant glare.

"No reason to suffer under this oppressive heat while we wait," he says.

"You'll get no argument from me," Vaughn happily agrees. Aimes and Blake make similar statements as we all crowd under the broad shadows of the Roc's wings.

Sinbad thrusts a skin of water to me, saying, "One should never neglect basic needs."

Amen to that! I think as I quickly gulp down half the skin before handing it back to him. He holds up his hand.

"Keep it. You'll need it more than I will."

We're right next to the shadow of the rock, giving us an excellent vantage point while we watch the sun climb higher into the sky. At first, we see nothing, and I wonder if I might be wrong again. But, then, all at once, it happens. A thin blue line spreads down the shadowed side of the rock, a bright shimmering azure that divides the rock right in front of us.

"There!" Blake says excitedly, pointing and running towards the space where the line ends. The sand slows his momentum, but he barely seems to notice.

Examining the line more closely, I detect a false surface, like a kind of laminate glued to the outside. Pulling the corner of it, Blake removes a flap. A parchment falls out onto the sand, its markings denoting it to be another map. The blue line remains visible for a second longer before disappearing again when the sun moves.

"Well done, Ember," Aimes says as he turns to face me with a big smile. "That was quite brilliant!"

"Quite brilliant," Sinbad repeats. "We are indeed lucky bastards." Then he apparently realizes I'm standing right there and bows. "I beg your pardon for my harsh language, dear lady."

I smile at him. "It's fine."

Blake hands the map to me. The sand creeps into every crack and crevice on my body, and the sun is bearing down on us, making it impossible for me to concentrate. A shadow suddenly shields us, and I look up in alarm. Thankfully, it's only the Roc, which moves closer and raises a wing in response to Sinbad's hand command.

"Better?" he asks.

"Much better," I reply as I examine the latest parchment. Everyone waits patiently while I study it for a few more minutes. This one has extensive notations that require more time to comprehend. When I look up again, Blake holds out the quill and Aimes offers me the inkpot. I quickly make the necessary markings before slowly untangling the cipher of the notation.

I frown when I finish. "This reads like very bad poetry."

"How so?" Aimes asks while capping the inkpot.

"Judge for yourself." I take a deep breath and recite the poem: "'A cave you will find and in it great wealth/But to lay hands on the treasure requires much stealth. Move past the magic/And the pits, oh so tragic. To fail could be bad for your health.'"

Sinbad makes a face like he's smelling a rotting corpse. "That *is* appalling."

"But what does it mean, exactly?" Blake asks.

"Well, I believe it means there's a cave full of treasures, guarded by traps and magic." I tap the markings I made. "It's got to be somewhere here in the Anoka Desert. But beyond that, it doesn't say where to find the entrance, and once we're inside the caves, where we should go."

"Perhaps the seeker within the cave is deprived the luxury of choice," Sinbad says.

"What does that even mean?" Vaughn barks with impatience.

"Simply this," Sinbad replies, unoffended. "A cave full of traps and pits and magic will likely determine where the traveler goes as well as what he..." He looks at me meaningfully before adding, "or *she* may or may not find."

"That doesn't sound very promising." I remark with a frown, imagining all the horrid places we might visit in the caves.

"No, it does not," Sinbad admits. "I truly hope I'm wrong, but that bit of badly composed verse suggests little else."

"Well, if one person can make it, someone else can break it," Blake says, interjecting himself into the conversation. He smiles at me. "I've every confidence you can get through whatever puzzles and magic we might encounter."

"Need I remind everyone that we still have one big problem?" I reply, shaking my head. "We don't know where these caves are."

Before anyone can respond, the wind begins to whirl ferociously around us. It quickly builds up into a sandstorm, pushing the grains of sand so hard through the air, not even the Roc's wings can stop it. There's no way the great bird can fly through this, never mind stay in place. We've come so close to our destination only for a freak sandstorm to stop us?

I can't deal with the onslaught of sand against my face and body any longer and my frustration makes me blurt out, "Just stop it!"

At my unexpected roar, the wind suddenly ceases and the swirling sand falls back to the ground. I'm as shocked as the others when an instant calm surrounds us.

"Ember?" Aimes asks.

I shake my head. "I don't... I don't understand what just..."

"If you were searching for proof of the fact that you're Chosen," Vaughn starts with a quick nod. "I believe you've just found it."

Several thoughts flash across my mind then:

Vaughn is right. The stone isn't wrong. I really must be one of the Chosen!

As I stand pondering the truth behind my own thoughts, words from the prophecy of the Chosen echo in my mind:

Bane of Madness,
She carves a stable path,
Guts the bull with its own horn,
And tramples the grapes of wrath.

A pang of dread swiftly replaces my amazement. Assuming those words apply to me, they can mean only one thing. I must confront Bacchus eventually. But, I feel no more prepared for that outcome than I did when we landed here.

CHAPTER THIRTEEN
AIMES

We fly at lower altitude, hopefully high enough to elude weapons from the ground but low enough to avoid unwanted attention. Dangers abound here, in my former home. Any number of clans will attack us if we're not careful. I wonder if my clan still survives in this harsh landscape. It's been a long time since I traversed these dunes, well before the war began. And I've been so busy fighting since then, I've forgotten how much I miss my home. Can I still even call it home?

"Do we even know where we're going?" Vaughn asks, interrupting my thoughts.

"Not unless someone spotted a cave full of treasures when I wasn't looking," Blake answers wearily. I have been studying him all this time, to ascertain how his health fares and based on the rosiness of what I would term his 'aura', I believe he is healing. As I'm unsure of the extent of the magic with which I was gifted, I'm pleased not to have to rely on it where Blake is concerned.

"What else can we do?" Vaughn asks.

"I have an idea," I say when I spot a familiar configuration of dunes and rocks on the horizon. "Point the bird that way, Sinbad."

"And what, pray tell, awaits us there?" Sinbad asks with an arched eyebrow.

"What he said," Vaughn grumbles. He sits with his arm clasped tightly around Ember and even though the visual stokes my internal fires of jealousy, I take comfort in the fact that at least she seems calm at the moment. If he can keep her that way until I'm able to clean her again, I shall be content.

"Hopefully, my clan awaits us. If they still survive, we can rest, get supplies, and figure out where we need to go next."

Blake gives me a dubious glance. "You've always preached that desert clans don't take well to outsiders."

"True, they still live by the old ways. That's why they have strict requirements for anyone to enter."

"Such as?" Ember asks, nakedly curious.

"For one, they won't allow us in with an unmarried woman," I reply.

The frown on Ember's face makes Sinbad say, "Such is the tyranny of the old ways, dear lady. It is why I refuse to live by them since I took the sea as my mistress."

"Then we'll have to shade the truth a little," Vaughn observes. "Who gets to be Ember's lucky husband?"

"Oh, all of us can be," I reply with a casual shrug.

The informality in my voice throws Ember off-guard, "What?"

"My clan is polyamorous," I reply with a shrug and a little smile.

"Poly-what-amous?" Vaughn asks.

"It means they believe in having multiple wives and husbands… the only requirements are equal love and equal support," I answer. Then I take a deep breath and face the other men in our group. "Since our mutual affection for our companion is quite obvious, it'll be best if they think we are all her husbands."

"I certainly have no problem with that," Sinbad pipes up.

I point at him. "Not you."

"Did you not just say—"

"Yes, but the Roc will be unwelcome under any circumstances. You'll have to stay outside my tribe's camp." I try to sweeten my statement a bit by adding, "Besides, didn't you say the sea is your only mistress?"

"Wonderful," Sinbad seethes with disgust. "Everyone else gets to enjoy Ember's charming company while I must sleep outside with my winged beast."

"If things go badly," Blake continues, "we'll need someone on the outside who can help us escape." The prince looks at me a bit self-consciously. "No disrespect to you or your tribe, Aimes."

"None taken," I assure him, then look over at Sinbad. "One of us will bring you and the Roc supplies as soon as we are able."

Sinbad shrugs his resignation as the Roc hovers over my clan's encampment. To my relief, the clan is still very much intact and inhabited, judging by the number of people pointing up at us. Thus, Hassan hasn't completely destroyed the people of the Anoka desert.

The Roc alights outside the large wooden gates and I climb down his feathered back, taking large steps until I reach the gates that surround my ancestral stronghold. I take a deep breath before grabbing one of the huge iron rings and rapping it violently against the wood. I don't even flinch as I hear the familiar sound of longbows being drawn overhead. Vaughn and Blake are immediately on guard, their swords poised and ready.

"Ease down, fellows," I say to the archers above us in a muffled voice. *"We shall pass while the sun is high, for tomorrow we know not if we may die."*

The password phrase successfully given, the archers lower their bows while the gates slowly open. Blake and Vaughn exchange a look while Ember studies the gates in wide-eyed wonder.

"Very cheerful pass phrase, that," Vaughn jokes.

"One of many. They change with the days of the week. I'm only glad I remembered today is Thursday."

"What if you remembered it wrong?" Ember asks.

"I wouldn't have gotten another chance to get it right."

"Comforting," Blake comments as the gates finish opening wide enough for us to file through. On the other side, we're met by a half-dozen people with scowls on their faces. The only exception is our leader, who gives us a neutral look.

"Aimes, my brother," he says, spreading his arms wide. "It's been too long since you came home."

We embrace and I say, "And yet to home, we must always return, Argos."

"Just so," Argos agrees with a friendly pat on the back. As we part, he asks, "So what brings you back after all these years?"

"My wife and her two husbands are on a mission," I explain.

"Wife?" Another man repeats while looking Ember up and down appreciatively. "We received no word of your nuptials."

"For which I can only apologize," I say with a bowed head.

"No, no, none of that," Argos admonishes me. "Due to the unfortunate state of the world, visitors are quite rare. Introducing me to your family is apology enough."

I smile and wave to the others. "My wife, Ember. Her two husbands, Blake and Vaughn." Then I wave back to our host and add, "May I introduce my brother, Argos."

A round of greetings later, Argos says, "I assume you all require a night's rest and supplies to continue your journey?"

"Where else in this part of the Anoka can a traveler find either luxury?" I ask rhetorically.

"And that appalling beast that our archers saw outside the gates? Will it remain there safely?" Argos asks.

"Our guide, Sinbad ensures it will," I reply.

Argos nods. "Well, since you've been married outside our walls, we must make your marriage official within the clan."

"Of course," I say, trying not to sound uneasy. The others may not like it, but if we want the clan's help, we need to do whatever is necessary to maintain the marriage illusion.

"Very good," Argos says, giving my shoulder a hearty clap. "We shall send a man to serve your guide and his beast a hearty meal with a bit of ale."

"He'll appreciate such kindness after our long journey."

Argos chuckles. "Yes, I imagine that great bird can shorten such a long trek." He looks at all of us. "But come now. Supper shall be ready soon and I would like to get you settled in."

We follow Argos to the inner encampment. I make introductions while hugging my brethren as we encounter them. Truly, nothing has changed here. Time stands still with my people, closed off from the world in their own little corner of the desert as they are. In some ways, that's good, comforting even. In an ever-changing world, it is always refreshing to find some things that don't. But everything outside this compound is different. And my clan are as unprepared now as they were when I left.

I'm surprised when they take us to my old tent, the one I lived in before I opted to travel. At my curious expression, Argos shrugs and says, "We knew you would return one day." Leaving the others behind, he and I gather supplies and catch up on the old and new.

While I can see how happy Argos is to see me, his disappointment that I can't stay eclipses his joy. He compensates by offering me far more supplies than I ask for. I protest that he's being too generous, but he will not hear of it.

"In what other way can I protect my brother from the perils he will likely face on the final leg of his quest?" he inquires.

I sigh as I hold up my hands. "Thank you, Argos. For everything."

"Come, come, brother," he admonishes me. "No need for thanks among family. Just return to us safely once more when you finish your quest. You always have a home here."

"I know," I reply, imagining my home and so many others that will be destroyed if Morningstar prevails.

Argos catches the look in my eyes. "Your mission... where does it take you?"

"We're not sure yet," I admit with a shrug. "We know it lies among the dunes, but we haven't managed to figure out exactly *where* among the dunes."

Argos nods and strokes his chin. "What can you tell me of it?"

Once I describe the clue we found in the crimson rock, he answers without hesitation. "Of course! The Caves of Larne."

"They actually exist?"

"Oh, yes. We found them at the desert's eastern edge several years ago."

"I remember the stories... the caves are full of treasure, but treacherous to pass."

"The stories are not wrong. No one who dares to enter the caves has ever returned." He puts a hand on my shoulder. "I should rethink this trek of yours, brother. Treasure might be precious, but life is priceless."

"It's not the riches we seek."

"Oh?"

I shake my head. "We must retrieve the Blue Faerie's wand. Without it, Hassan will end us all."

"Hassan," Argos sneers, turning the name into a curse. "May the nine hells retrieve his black soul for a plaything. If that coward dares to venture onto our land, I will gladly end his life myself."

"And perhaps that's why he doesn't."

Argos chuckles again. "Perhaps." He pauses. "I can tell you where to find the caves, but beyond that, I'm afraid I can't help you, my brother. May your companions suffice to navigate its pitfalls."

I nod because I understand. "Thank you, Argos."

We finish loading the supplies on a cart. When the sun rises again, they'll be transported to the Roc. In the meantime, a maid is sent to deliver food, ale and any other pleasure Sinbad might request. Perhaps he won't be so displeased to be left out after all.

I return to the tent and I'm not pleased to see a pair of my clansmen watching the tent as I pass it—they're suspicious of outsiders and I knew such would be the case, but that doesn't mean I like it. Yet my comrades seem relaxed, shaking the sand out of their clothes and hair.

"I'm sorry about this," I tell them upon entering the tent. "Treating you like strangers and sticking you under guard in this tent like common hostages is hardly my idea of hospitality."

"Nothing to worry about," Blake tells me.

"It'll be nice to rest beyond the shelter of that damned Roc's wings," Vaughn adds.

"Well, shall we eat?" I ask.

"Yes, please, I'm starving," Ember says, quickly rising to her feet.

Small wonder. The pomegranates were all we ate since last night. I'm impressed Sinbad brought enough food for his bird to fly us this far.

"Before we go, we need to talk about our upcoming nuptials," I say on a sigh.

"How do these nuptials of ours work exactly?" Vaughn asks with the kind of eagerness he usually shows before a good fight.

I tell them about the ritual we must perform on the mountain after our meal. In conclusion, I say, "I know this seems unnecessary, but it will make the difference in whether or not the clan accepts you as family and… I believe we will need their help when the time comes." I clear my throat as I look at Ember. "And, of course, a marriage in my clan doesn't mean we will be married… according to society."

Blake and Vaughn nod their assent. Then we all look toward Ember. After a moment, she gives us a smile.

"I understand the reasons why," she says, walking towards me. She nods and seems to gather all her strength. "Now that I know I have a greater purpose than the pathetic, little existence I've been trapped in…

I realize I must rely on not just myself, but others." She pauses. "All of you."

I realize she must be referring to the fact that she's one of the Chosen, something that still strikes me as incredible, and yet it isn't unbelievable. Ember's abilities might not be physically embodied, the way the abilities of the others have proven thus far. Ember's abilities are all in her head.

She stands in the middle of all of us and laughs. "Of course, I'm scared witless about what lies ahead."

"We will be with you every step of the way," Blake says softly.

She turns to face him and nods. "I know I can get through anything with all of you by my side." I don't know when she's had this change of heart, but I imagine it has everything to do with the moment she first found out she was Chosen. As to her relationship with Blake, it's still on faulty ground, but it does seem as if she's softening towards him. Maybe not as much as she's softened with Vaughn and me, but their relationship doesn't seem fraught with so much bad blood as it once did.

"Anyway, I'm really hungry." She practically skips out of the tent, calling to us, "Let's go eat."

We all look at one another for a moment. "You heard the lady... our *wife*," Vaughn quips. We all have to laugh as we follow her out.

###

The four of us join the clan around the large fire for the evening meal.

We eat heartily while some of our talented youth perform a tribal dance. When they finish, they trot off to eat their suppers while the adults pass around tankards of strong ale to cleanse our palettes.

"Shall we begin the marriage ritual?" one of the elders finally asks. In response, I stand up and say, "One sun sets and a new one rises."

We proceed to the mountain, and the elder who spoke first conducts the ritual. He ties knots made of various swaths of silk around each of our hands, connecting each of ours to Ember's. When the ritual concludes, I take Ember's hand in mine before pulling her close.

"Can I kiss you?" I whisper.

She simply nods, so I pull her even closer, then I kiss her passionately for all to see, prompting enthusiastic whoops and applause. Although our marriage may be false, a harsh punishment would result if we fail to convince our clan it's real.

When I release her, she's blushing madly and drops the line of her eyes to the floor.

"I believe it's my turn," Vaughn says as he steps forward and Ember turns to face him. She swallows hard and I can see she's nervous—proof is in her fidgeting hands and the blush pinkening her cheeks. She simply nods up at Vaughn and he responds by lifting her off her feet as he plants a deep kiss on her lips. She wraps her arms around him and furthers the kiss and I suddenly feel as if the one the two of us shared pales in comparison. It just… had none of the vigor this one does.

Blake then steps up to Vaughn and taps him on the shoulder, causing the bigger man to disengage from Ember and step back. Yet, his eyes are on her the entire time and I can see by his breeches that he's hard. He wants her just as much as I want her—just as much as all three of us want her. Well, Sinbad too, for that matter. I've seen his own expressions of longing.

Blake approaches Ember and they both just stand there for a moment. Then he reaches out and takes her hand, bending low as he brings it to his lips. I hope he doesn't think this will suffice as a nuptial kiss. Seconds later, he stands up and whispers something in her ear, no doubt asking for her consent, and she nods. Moments later, he's whisked her into his arms and his lips are on hers. The kiss is shorter than either Vaughn's or mine. But that matters not for we've accomplished what the clan wanted us to. We're married. All four of us.

Ember pauses and then smiles at my elders, who watch, stone-faced and seemingly unimpressed. I warned her such might be the case.

"Now, if you'll all excuse us, we'll continue our affection in private," Vaughn tells them as Ember's cheeks grow an even darker shade of red. Without another word, he lifts Ember into his arms and starts back the way we came, pulling the rest of us with him, by our knotted hands.

"Do you think they bought it?" Vaughn asks once we're inside our tent. The clansmen have long since departed.

"We'll learn the hard way if they didn't," I reply, unravelling the knots around our wrists. I look at Ember and smile. "You did a good job."

"Thank... thank you," she answers and appears to be completely uncomfortable.

"Ember, you know this doesn't mean we have to," I start.

"Of course not," Blake interrupts. "We would never expect you to feel like you had to... lay with us."

"It was just a marriage for show," Vaughn adds.

Ember nods but then chews on her lower lip and it appears her brain is busily pondering something. She looks up at me and then the other two, still chewing her lower lip. "What if..." she starts and then seems to lose her nerve.

"What if?" I prod her.

She looks back at me and nods, apparently stealing her courage again. "What if... I *wanted* to understand what... physical love feels like?"

Neither of us responds right away. I think we're all too dumbfounded to know what to say. It's finally Vaughn who steps forward and takes her hand.

"Then we would have to show you, wouldn't we?"

Ember nods and then looks up at all three of us. "I haven't... I've never... been with a man before."

And then I suddenly realize what we're about to do—what she's asking us to do. And, yet, she's never been with a man before? Now she's with three? For her very first time? It just... it doesn't seem right.

"I don't," I start, shaking my head as I look from Blake to Vaughn. "I don't know that this is the right thing to do."

"I don't think it is either," says Blake, and I'm surprised.

"Don't... don't you want me?" Ember asks quietly.

"Of course we want you, Dove," Vaughn says as he reaches out and runs his fingers down her face. "But not because we've been roped into a fake wedding."

"I don't... I don't understand," she says.

"Love between a man and a woman or three men and a woman," I correct with a laugh, "needs to be just that—love," I try to explain. "And I think the point we're trying to make is that we want you to fully want us." I look up at the other two and they nod their agreement, so I continue. "We don't want you to feel like you have to do this, owing to... the situation."

"I don't feel like that," she argues. "In our travels, I've begun to trust you." She looks at Blake then. "All of you. And I... I can't think of any other men who would be better to introduce me to... physical love."

I approach, and she smiles as I pull her into a kiss. My mouth covers hers and I can feel her heart beating rapidly.

"We will never hurt you," I whisper. "We will always care for you and protect you... no matter what."

"I know," she whispers as I push her down to the floor of the tent. Then I look back up at Blake and

Vaughn. "We need to take our time with her," I say. "One step at a time."

Blake nods. "This is your time, Aimes," he says.

"But do you mind if we watch?" Vaughn asks on a chuckle.

"Ember?" I ask her.

She looks up at all three of us. "I want all of you here."

I run my fingers down the side of her face, taking my time, enjoying her smooth skin. I'm eager to bury my cock deep inside her, making her at least partly mine. But, I'm not going to allow that to happen. Not now anyway. For now, I just want her to experience something—the first step in the art of lovemaking. And when she decides she wants me or all of us to take residence inside her fully, that will be her decision to make. After she's thought about it.

For now, I want to give her pleasure, so I unbutton her trousers and pull them down the long line of her legs. Then, when her panties are all that separates me from her sex, I slip them aside and reach between her legs, sliding my thumb lightly across her hardened nub. I feel her shiver and moan into my mouth as I create the slightest friction on her clit.

"May I?" Blake asks as he leans down and makes a motion as if he wants to unbutton her blouse. She nods at him and when all that's left is her brassiere, he expertly removes it. All the while, I continue my ministrations on her hardened nub, dipping down into the hollow of her sex to wet my finger. Oh, how I absolutely want to seat myself within her, but I won't allow it. Not at this moment, at any rate.

For now, this moment—it's all about Ember.

I pull my lips away to focus on her perfect breasts and suckle one of her pale pink nipples, letting it harden under my tongue as I continue to tease her clit with my thumb and fingers. Blake, meanwhile, titillates her other nipple and Vaughn reaches down to insert the tip of his finger into her dripping center. She arches up against him, eager for more, so he pushes his finger inside her deeper—up to his knuckle.

I forget everything but her as I gently kiss the tops of her mounds, slipping my finger inside her slick folds, beside Vaughn's, as she coos into my hair.

"Goddess below, you're so beautiful," I tell her, increasing the movements of my hand as she quivers against me. I can feel her body responding as she approaches orgasm, the tightness of her soft folds closing around our fingers, pulsating across my skin.

Quickening our pace, Vaughn and I increase the rhythm of our fingers, pushing them inside her all the way up as far as our fingers will go and then pulling them out again.

"She's soaking wet," Blake says.

"And incredibly tight," Vaughn answers.

The three of us are beyond turned on and yet not one of us attempts to take control of the situation. Instead, we allow her to squirm beneath us as we fuck her with our fingers. A moment or so later, she cries out with pleasure. Her body keeps rising and falling with our combined movements, nearly impaling herself on our hands. Finally she lets loose with an orgasm so powerful, it racks her entire body, her juices flowing down our hands in a hot gush. I can feel her walls contracting two more times before she's finally spent.

We remain there for a moment, my mouth once again covering hers as I kiss her with more passion than I've ever felt with another woman.

CHAPTER FOURTEEN
EMBER

I'm not anxious to resume our journey again.

Last night, experiencing what I did with Aimes, Blake and Vaughn... I can't stop thinking about it and every time I do, a blush steals across my cheeks. I was just so... so wanton! So naughty! And, truthfully, I want to do the same again... the same and more.

As we ride the Roc over the parched desert, I try to get the memory of last night's activity out of my head. But I can't keep the memory of the three of them touching me or the way their eyes settled on the valley between my legs. I can only wonder what it must be like to have them fully seated within me.

I clench my thighs when a familiar sensation vibrates between my legs. It reminds me of how soiled I am now, causing my anxiety to rear its ugly head. Oddly, what we did together doesn't feel dirty to me. Everything was magical, passionate, perfect even.

Flying across the desert does make me feel dirty, though, when the sand below us seems to be everywhere. I feel anxious and begin to fidget. I almost ask Sinbad to land the Roc so Aimes can clean me properly. But I don't know how long until we arrive at the caves. Since we must be prepared for anything as we travel, it's not the best idea right now.

So I turn to math exercises. I count by threes as the Roc glides quietly above the desert floor. *Three, six, nine, twelve...* By the time we arrive at the caves, I've lost my count.

"So this is it?" Vaughn asks, jumping off the Roc as the great bird comes to rest at the cave's entrance. He turns toward me and holds out his arms to steady me as I disembark from the monstrous bird.

"Argos wouldn't steer us anywhere else," Aimes assures him when he and Blake jump down on either side of me. Sinbad tosses down some of the supplies: weapons, snacks and canteens of water. Though mine is almost empty, I don't complain. I know how to make do.

Aimes's clan knows little about the caves, an inevitable consequence since no one has ever come out of them alive. Thus, we have no way of knowing what to expect. Sinbad hops off the Roc before guiding the creature to one side. He says something quietly into the bird's ear and it lies down, facing the entrance to the cave.

"He shall wait for us," Sinbad says, patting the Roc's beak. "And none will enter behind us." He glances at the dark maw of the cave. "Such a pity he can do nothing to help us against whatever traps await us inside."

"At least we won't have to worry about any uninvited guests," Aimes says, forever the optimist.

Sinbad nods before looking at me thoughtfully. "Are you certain you want the lady to travel with us?"

I bristle at that. I've ridden countless miles on the back of Sinbad's monster bird and now he thinks I'm unfit for the remainder of our journey?

Thankfully, Blake steps in. "Ember's the only one who can discern the ciphers."

"Are we not done with ciphers at this point?" Sinbad inquires. "Won't the wand be protected by a means far more… physical?"

"Without a doubt," Blake agrees. "But for all we know, the wand can only be retrieved by understanding one final cipher. Best to plan for that now than be sorry later."

"And I wouldn't feel good leaving her by herself," Vaughn adds, to which the other men nod.

Sinbad's expression is slightly regretful. "Then may we emerge with the wand in hand."

"We shall," Vaughn replies triumphantly. "Whatever it takes."

Aimes claps his hands together. "Well, no time like the present. Shall we?"

I nod. "We shall!"

The five of us begin walking toward the cave. When we hit the opening, my heart starts thudding against my breast as twenty or so steps in, the light disappears, giving way to darkness. We stop to light the small torches we've brought with us before looking around. Nothing appears to be out of the ordinary and as far as I can tell, there's nothing of interest: no cave markings, glyphs or anything else. The walls are covered with leaves, dried vines and twigs stuck together with mud.

We know from Aimes's clan that such is misleading. The cave purposely seems like any other until it doesn't. According to Argos, the cave swallows men whole, cuts them in half, drowns them and pushes them out its inner walls. And those are just the men they've found! We proceed with great caution, inching our way along while watching for signs of booby-trapped doors, barbs, tripwires, and anything else that might harm us.

Things seem to be going well when a sudden breeze rises out of nowhere. Before we can react, it sucks us downward, making the floor vanish beneath our feet and sending us all down several tunnels. I scream as I'm swallowed into the earth, and suddenly falling without end. I lose my grip on the torch, which winds up falling ahead of me. I hear it getting doused by water, but it's water I can't see. I try to prepare myself for the worst. How ironic to drown in a cave right in the middle of the desert!

Finally, I hit the water and going under, fight to right myself. Swimming upward, my head clears the water and once I'm able to stand, I find the water is only waist deep. Blake lands beside me, holding his torch high above his head. I grab it before it submerges with him. While the torch casts some light around us, we still can't see very much. And I can't imagine that's a good thing.

CHAPTER FIFTEEN
BLAKE

While Ember and I take stock of our surroundings, I feel the floor beneath us shifting. Holding the torch higher to cast as much light as possible around us, I try to see what's happening. When Ember moves toward me, the ground shifts again.

She looks down at her body, submerged just above waist height. Her eyes grow wide when the water creeps up another inch as we watch it.

"The water's getting deeper every time we move," she says, looking back at me.

"So let's not move," I reply, bringing the torch closer to the rising liquid. It's incredibly clear, enough to allow me to see a series of symbols set in tile. The tiles look as though they can be pushed.

"What is this place?" Ember asks.

"I don't know, but I think we need to figure out what these glyphs mean if we want to find a way out."

We both look at the puzzle as the waters gradually rise. To my eyes, they're only a series of random symbols. "Is this some sort of cipher?" I ask her.

"I don't think so," she says, shaking her head. "I can't see any pattern to it. Each symbol is different to the next, so there's nothing to match together."

"A language, perhaps?"

"None that I've ever seen before."

I can tell from the tremble in her voice that she's getting anxious. I'm not sure I can calm her down because she's just out of my reach. And taking any steps toward her will surely make the water rise again. So I lower the torch and that's when I notice something moving beneath the water. With my light so close to the surface, Ember sees it too.

"What is that?" she gasps in panic.

I look closer and finally manage to make one of the creatures out.

"Phantom piraya."

"Oh no!" she gasps, nearly hyperventilating.

"It's all right," I tell her, knowing my words won't calm her. "They're well below us, see?"

She leans over and sees the little flesh-seeking bastards are quite far below, beneath the tiles. "They're close, though," she answers. "Too close."

I can't disagree. While I'm a fairly brave man, the thought of being eaten alive by ghostly white carnivores makes my skin crawl.

"Just stay calm, Ember. They're still quite far away from us."

"For now," she says quietly. The gravity of our situation is obviously sinking in, proportionate to the increased level of her panic. "But this floor keeps dropping, which brings them closer."

"Yes," I reply, not trusting myself to say more.

An epiphany appears in her eyes. "I think I understand now," she says, nodding. "We have to solve the puzzle. And I imagine each time we get the solution incorrect, the floor drops deeper into the water below."

"And if the floor gets too low, we'll have to contend with the piraya."

"Yes," she says as she looks back down at the tiles and studies them in silent deliberation. Finally, she looks back at me again. "We must move from one correct stone to the next."

"How can we tell which ones are correct, though?"

She looks closer at the tiles. "Those symbols aren't painted. They're holes."

The floor shifts again, and Ember lets out a scream while looking at me with wild eyes. I clench my jaw, remarking, "Apparently, we don't have forever to figure this out."

"I can't do it," she gasps. "Oh gods and goddesses! I can't do this."

"Yes, you can, Ember," I reassure her. "You've solved much more difficult puzzles than this one. This is your purpose. You know you can do it."

"I don't even know where to start," she babbles, shaking her head. "And every wrong step gets us closer to those… awful things below us."

"I have all the faith in the world in you, Ember," I say as she looks up at me with those large green eyes. "Now, you need to have faith in yourself."

She takes a deep breath and nods, staring down into the water, her eyes flitting from one stone to the next. I hold up my torch to illuminate the area as best I can. The walls around us look solid, no exit in sight. I assume that solving the puzzle will send us upward again.

"I've got it!" she squeals suddenly. "It's a puzzle."

"Didn't we already figure that much out?" I ask, disappointed.

"I mean, it's like a jigsaw puzzle. All the pieces are really odd shapes that can only fit together in one particular way."

"So how do we move them?"

"We don't. We move *ourselves*." When she sees my confusion, she explains, "We go from one puzzle piece to the next until we complete the puzzle. We have to move from one correct piece to the next correct piece that fits into it. If we make a wrong move, the floor drops."

The last part sounds ominous, but at least we have a plan. "So, where do we start?"

"Right where I'm standing. I'll move to the next piece that fits."

"Then should I follow you?"

"No, it's best if you stay right where you are. Otherwise, we might cancel each other's progress."

I nod, feeling an impending sense of doom. No wonder no one ever gets out of this place. Even if Ember's right, what's to stop her from being ejected somewhere away from me, or catapulted into another puzzle or trap?

I lean forward and hand her the torch. "I can't take your only source of light," she protests.

"You need it more than I do right now," I point out. Reluctantly, she takes the torch before staring at the tiles beneath her feet.

She can do this. She's strong. She's a Chosen One. She can get us out of here. At least, I hope she can, for both our sakes. My nerves are ragged as I watch and wait.

She moves slowly, quietly, and further away from me. As the torchlight recedes, I'm left in the darkness, hearing only small, almost inaudible clicks each time she moves from one stone to the next. It sounds like some sort of mechanism clicking within the chamber, hopefully unlocking an exit.

I brace myself for any mistake, calculating how long it might take for the floor to slip down into the piraya tank. Once we get low enough, will the divider between us just retract, letting those little bastards slip out of their holes to devour us? The phantom piraya are a particularly nasty variety of predator, eating everything they can, even bones. I can't begin to fathom how many men could have ended up between their steely razor teeth over the years.

I can barely make out Ember's silhouette as she stands at the edge of the floor, nearest the wall. She takes another step to one side. A loud click sounds, and the floor suddenly lurches downward. My heart sinks, but just as quickly, the floor begins to rise, snapping itself into place above the water, and sealing all the holes. A section of the chamber wall begins to slide open.

"Run!" Ember yells.

I don't hesitate, sprinting towards her while a series of clicks sound beneath my feet and the floor begins to reset. I reach her just before the floor drops again. We both throw ourselves through the opening.

She screams when I grab her and slam her against the wall next to our exit, flattening myself beside her. A series of spinning blades come within inches of our faces, one of them narrowly missing her as she stumbles through the door.

After catching our collective breath, we stay put, allowing our heartbeats to calm as the chamber behind us closes once again. The blades never stop swinging above us.

CHAPTER SIXTEEN
AIMES

The trap door opens into two tunnels.

Looking around, I see Vaughn and Sinbad have landed in this one with me. Blake and Ember are missing, so I have to assume they fell into the other one.

I hold my torch up high, and watch as Sinbad kneels to pick up one of the other lit torches, where it burns on the ground, before handing it to Vaughn. Vaughn uses it to relight the third, which extinguished itself on the way down. He hands the torch back to Sinbad. With fire in our hands to light our way, we look around to determine where we are. There's only one tunnel leading away from the open room.

"I guess we're going that way," I say, pointing toward it.

"Brilliant deduction," Vaughn grumbles as he starts walking.

As we approach the corridor, a cat appears to be prowling back and forth in front of the exit, stopping in front of us when we get near. Odd enough for any creature to be down here, and upon further inspection, this one appears to be made of wood. We all examine it warily. Is it a trap?

"What is two plus two?" it asks in a mechanical tone.

"Why the fuck is a cat asking us such a stupid question?" Vaughn retorts.

Immediately, the cat's blue-jeweled eyes click shut and pop back open, except now they're red. It turns toward the sound of Vaughn's voice, emitting a high-pitched howl, followed by one word, "Wrong!"

Without warning, the cat's tail pops upward and curls into a U-shape over its back. A small barb shoots out and pierces Vaughn's shin. He curses, reaching down to pull the barb free. Holding it up briefly, he casts it aside.

"What is two plus two?" the cat repeats.

Vaughn moves toward the thing, meaning to kick it down the tunnel. But it rears up on its back two feet and hisses at him. He stops dead in his tracks, readying himself for the attack. Fearing this could escalate into something much worse than a mere barb, I intervene by shouting, "Four! The answer is four!"

The cat settles on the floor again, its blue eyes snapping back into place. Then it moves out of our way and lies quietly beside the wall.

"This reeks of the madness in Wonderland," Sinbad remarks as we begin to move forward.

"Not a comforting thought," I say, shivering at the other unwholesome things that come from there.

"Sure would explain that pissed-off pussycat, though," Vaughn says, limping painfully on his injured leg. Blood is already coursing down his leg and pooling in his shoe. From the looks of it, though, it's just a surface injury.

Only a few feet in, we encounter another cat blocking our path. This one is made from metal and its shining, bejeweled eyes are similar to those of the wooden one. We stop and wait for it to speak. I'm expecting another ridiculous math question, but that's not what we get.

"Where would one go to order a special Christmas pie in Sweetland?" it asks.

Vaughn steps forward and answers with slightly slurred speech. "The Minishterr of Merry Minnce in the Peppermint Panntryy."

"Correct!" the cat exclaims, moving to one side to allow us through.

As we keep walking, I ask Vaughn, "How did you know the answer to such an odd question?"

"Emberr."

"Um," I start, frowning at his sudden lisp.

"Havth you thnot been listhening to herr?"

I study him with a frown. "I have, but she talks about numerous subjects when we travel. I'm afraid I've forgotten some of it." Then I give him a critical eye. "You sound rather odd, Vaughn. Are you okay?"

He gives me a funny look. "Yeth, twhy?"

"Has your tongue gone numb?" Sinbad asks.

Vaughn smacks his lips together, sticking his tongue out a couple of times, as though to test it. He furrows his brow and looks back at us. "Yeth. Ith iss."

Sinbad appears unsurprised. "Just as I feared... that barb was drugged."

143

"With whath?" Vaughn slurs.

"If my Wonderland guess is correct, something unpleasant."

"And if you're experiencing that much numbness from such a tiny dose," I add, "you don't want to get struck by more of them."

"Thit," Vaughn says.

"Let's get through these blasted riddles and get out of here," I offer, moving ahead of both of them. It's not long before a third cat, made of fine glass, halts our progress. This one is bigger than the others and transparent, displaying its inner gears.

"I offer you a riddle," it says. "You have me today and tomorrow you'll have more. As time passes on, I'm more difficult to store. I don't take up space, dwell in only one place. What am I?"

The three of us look at each other in puzzlement. Of all the times to be without Ember's probing intellect… I rack my brain, trying to remember the answer to every riddle I've ever heard. Then it hits me.

"You're a memory!" I blurt out, preparing to dodge whatever emerges from the glass beast in front of us. But all it does is walk toward the wall and sit quietly as we pass.

"Geppetto designed these wretched things," Sinbad comments.

"What makes you so sure?" I ask him.

"I had a good view of that last one's craftsmanship. No one does work like that but him."

"Theth quethionth ur getthin hardurr," Vaughn comments, his tongue growing thicker.

144

"And your speech impediment is getting worse, old friend," I point out. "Best to let Sinbad and I answer until that barb wears off."

He grunts and we continue forward, preparing for the next cat. Sure enough, only a few feet ahead, another one appears, once again, bigger than the last. This one is a mixture of metal, glass and wood, quite exquisite in its creation and most likely, just as deadly. Sinbad's guess that Geppetto is the designer makes quite a lot of sense.

What I don't understand is why he'd do such a thing? Did someone in Wonderland force him to? Or is he as mad as the Hatter? Maybe he didn't realize what he was creating?

The cat then asks me, "Eleven plus two equals one. What does nine plus five equal?"

Vaughn flashes ten fingers, then four more but I shake my head no. That would be too easy. Besides, eleven plus two equals thirteen. In what instance could it equal one? And how does it relate to the second equation?

Sinbad glances at his wrist and smiles before practically shouting the answer. "Two!"

The cat instantly moves aside and lies down. Vaughn and I both look at him with a curious expression. He shrugs.

"Vaughn is not the only one who learned from your charming bride on our way over."

"Explain," I say.

Sinbad shrugs. "She showed us diverse ways to look at numbers because she counts so much to keep

145

herself calm. At one point, she talked about counting by the clock. Thus, eleven o'clock plus two hours equals one o'clock."

"And nine o'clock plus five hours equals two o'clock," I say, thinking of the clock tower in Sweetland. "Amazing. She saved our asses twice without even being here with us."

Our sense of triumph is quickly doused by the increasingly larger cats and their increasingly complex riddles. Somehow, we muddle through them. Vaughn even participates again after the poison fades from his system and his speech returns to normal.

"Fuck me." he half whispers, half hisses when the next cat comes into sight in the distance. "How many more of these bastards can there be, and how big can they get?" This one is made of black metal with bright yellow eyes. Designed to look like a panther, it stands at least a head taller than any of us.

We're quiet as we approach it, and my heart is racing. The eager expressions on our faces fall as it asks its question. We silently concur that our luck is about to run out. Any answer we give is likely to seal our doom.

"What brought you here, friends?" it asks innocently.

The three of us stand there, contemplating the best answer. Racking my own brain, I conclude I have no idea what's in this cave besides the Blue Faerie's wand. If we admit such is what we're looking for, there's a good chance we might be killed. I gesture for the others to move aside. The only thing we can do now is answer honestly and try to avoid whatever consequences await us.

Both of them refuse to budge, shaking their heads. I glare at them, but understand. Still, one wrong word and we're all toast. I look back at the cat, noting how its eyes are already beginning to darken, going from yellow to orange. Red can't be too far away. I'm ready to tell the truth and hoping for the best when Sinbad suddenly blurts out, "Our legs!"

Much to my surprise, the cat's eyes go dark without moving or attacking. It just sits in the corridor's center, blocking our way. We have to squeeze together to get around it.

I look at Sinbad with surprise. "How in the nine bloody hells did you figure that out?"

"Geppetto," he explains. "I was once told a story by a relative of Mastro Antonio about that old man's bad disposition. When he came to visit one day, Mastro Antonio asked what brought him there."

"And I'm guessing he said, 'my legs'?"

He points and nods. "So if Geppetto really did make these things, it would follow that at least one of them would have to contain a gem of his wit."

"Helluva guess," Vaughn says.

"True, but far less dangerous than any other answer."

"True enough," I admit. "All right, let's see how much bigger the next cat is."

The corridor begins to bend upward toward a set of large metal doors. No cats are in sight, thank the stars above. For a moment, I dare to hope this may be the end of our nightmare. But, just before we reach the doors, a metal woman steps out. The handles to the doors seem to be imbedded side-by-side with her in the center, blocking our way. We stop short, expecting one last question to be asked.

"You are not wanted here," she says in a mechanical tone.

"Not wanted by whom, you?" Vaughn snaps. "You're nothing but some scrap metal and gears."

"That may be how I appear to you, but such is not what I am."

"Then what are you?" I ask.

"Inside my chest, there's a stone that contains the soul of a witch. That's how I can converse with you. I am able to think, something I've had plenty of time to do."

"That may well be," Sinbad says. "But our business lies beyond your doors, metal maiden. I ask you to let us through."

Her head turns slightly toward him as a soft whir sounds through the corridor. Her eyes, made of aquamarine stones, turn in tiny sections to focus on him. There's a moment of silence before she speaks again.

"You will never see to your business, Sinbad of the Seven Seas," she says. "If you do not turn around and leave, you will meet your death inside these caves."

"How do you know my name?" he asks, squinting suspiciously at her.

"That is unimportant."

"My mission here is anything but unimportant," Sinbad replies. "Should I fail, I shall lose my entire clan."

"If you do not leave, you shall lose your life. And your clan will remain prisoners, regardless. Understand you cannot possess that which you seek."

Sinbad's eyes grow furious. "And who are you to say what I can and cannot do?"

"It is not by my will that this is so, you fool," the metal woman tells him. "None but a faerie can survive a wand's power when wielded. A mere mortal such as yourself would perish the moment you laid your hands on it."

The three of us look at one another with the same silent question: is she telling the truth? Still, truth or not, it changes nothing.

"We will continue our quest," I say to the mechanical woman.

"Does this man speak for you?" the metal witch asks, her gaze still settled on Sinbad.

"On this matter, he does," Sinbad says.

She grunts as she steps to one side. "Then so may you may enter."

She pushes a button in her palm that opens the doors. The moment we step through them, we find ourselves face-to-face with an enormous golden lion that blocks the way to yet another set of doors.

The doors behind us slam shut with a final clang.

"Well," Vaughn mutters as he looks at the lion. "Fuck me."

CHAPTER SEVENTEEN
EMBER

"Don't look down," Blake cautions when we plaster ourselves against the wall behind us. I can't resist although I instantly become woozy while staring into the deep, black chasm below us. Blake protectively puts his arm around me and I look away. Gray swirls of fog suddenly become visible. They grow increasingly darker as they descend, ultimately leaving nothing but blackness.

"Hello?" I call into the void. I receive no reply, not even an echo.

"What are you doing?" Blake asks.

"I hoped I could tell how deep it was by the sound of my echo."

"There was no echo."

"Exactly. So, I wonder just how deep it could be?"

"I really don't want to know," he replies, eyeing the sharp blades that continue to spin randomly around the room. They come dangerously close to us occasionally, but the wall provides some safety.

I look slowly around, afraid to move. The ledge we're perched on doesn't extend far enough, offering no chance of carefully creeping around to the other side, where I can see a door. In fact, the tiny ledge is part of the door we just came through. Suddenly I tense with fear: if someone happened along—meaning, they managed to solve the same puzzle I just did—and opened the door, we'd no doubt spiral helplessly into the abyss below. I reach for the empty canteen strapped to my side, but Blake shakes his head.

"I don't think you can put that up to your mouth without getting your hand caught by one of the blades," he warns me.

"It's empty." Snapping the strap off, I let it fall.

We stand still, listening and waiting. The canteen is old, heavy and made of metal. I expect it to make some sort of sound, but there's nothing. The abyss is either extremely deep or even bottomless.

"Not good," Blake observes.

"Very, very bad, I'd say."

He takes an unsteady breath. "Okay. Let's consider our options."

I do my own brief survey. "There aren't any anchor points on the walls that would allow us enough footing to edge around. It's too far to jump across and last time I checked, neither of us can fly."

"I certainly can't," Blake confirms. "But even if I could, how likely is it that I'd be able to dodge all those blades?"

I examine them more closely and a lightbulb goes off in my head. "Maybe we can use the blades to our advantage and swing across?"

Blake grunts and shakes his head. "If we could detect a pattern to their movement, that might allow us to wrap our hands around them..." Then he adds, "And we'd have to pray they could hold our weight."

"Let's see if I can accomplish the first part," I say, studying the blades more carefully.

I stare at them for what seems like hours but is really only minutes. I watch them move around, errantly unattached to anything solid, barely avoiding one another like drunken flies performing a haphazard dance.

"If there's a pattern, I don't see it," I finally say, loath to admit defeat.

"Any other ideas?"

"Is it too late to go back in time and not enter this gods-forsaken cave?"

"I wish that were possible. But the one person who might help us to do so isn't here."

The oblique mention of Aimes instantly saddens me. Where are he and the others? Are they even still alive? And, if so, what perils did the trap door subject them to when they dropped into the other tunnel?

"Do you think Aimes could accomplish such a magical feat?" I ask.

Blake shrugs. "I don't know. I don't even think he knows. But, it remains that his magic has helped us out of a bind more than once and he continuously uses it on you."

I nod and I'm suddenly reminded of the sandstorm near the rock, though I don't know why. When the wind storm was whipping up around us and threatening to suck us into it, I worried we'd end up miles apart, only to slowly dry up and die alone.

Something stirs inside me and I yell, "That's it!"

"What?" Blake replies, startled by my unexpected epiphany.

"Remember when I stopped the sandstorm?"

"These blades aren't the same as grains of sand, Ember."

"But they're flying objects. The sand was flying too. Until I calmed it."

"What do you mean?"

Rather than answering him, I stare hard at the blades and command, "Stop at once!"

At my stern directive, the blades immediately stop and hover very low in front of us. They're far too sharp to handle, as I suggested earlier. But they do look quite sturdy as Blake hoped, and another idea pops into my mind.

Balancing with one hand, I raise the other and motion for the blades to come together. In a few moments, they lie flat and their sharp edges no longer pose any danger. The impromptu road of metal extends from one end of the space to the other.

Blake carefully taps the makeshift bridge with his toe. "Will it hold us?"

"I don't know," I reply. "But let's find out before they start flying again."

He nods and braces himself. "Three... two... one..."

We jump onto the blades and race across the chasm. I hold my breath the whole time, as they shift and move beneath my feet with every footfall. The blades feel so wobbly and unpredictable, like they could fall apart any second, plunging us into darkness forever. To my happy amazement, though, they sustain us until we reach the doors on the opposite side. The doors swing open and the two of us jump through.

"Dear gods and goddesses," Blake says, exhaling with relief.

Instead of flying blades and a bottomless abyss, we find ourselves standing in a spacious room where I view the largest treasure trove I've ever seen. Of course, I've never seen any treasure before, but this still has to be the largest in existence. From one wall to the other, countless gold coins, trinkets, and jewels carpet the floor. Exquisite statues and rare artwork in heavy frames are scattered about the room or nestled among crowns, scepters and even a few thrones. All the items feature infinite amounts of precious gems and metals.

As we marvel at the unexpected sight, I notice something else on the other side of the room, something dark and sinister. Blake and I exchange a look before joining hands.

"Maybe it's another cave trick," Blake grumbles.

"Or a sentry guarding the treasure," I suggest. When your family tree has lots of dragons in it, that's the first possibility to consider. And my family tree is full of dragons.

I pray I'm wrong. Instead, I hope whatever awaits us is just another means of deterring intruders from the treasure. Nonetheless, I shudder at the thought of my first guess being correct.

CHAPTER EIGHTEEN
VAUGHN

To our surprise, a male lion, that appears to be neither real nor mechanical, begins to speak. I can't help but wonder could a real lion be standing before us? After all those damned cats, anything seems possible.

"I will choose one of you to answer the last riddle," the lion says. His voice sounds like a cross between a storm cloud and an angry god. "If you fail to answer the riddle correctly, you will meet a painful end. If you answer correctly, you may continue your quest."

We all wait, each of us clearly afraid to speak. After my previous dose of poison, I shudder to think what this creature might do to us. I pray to anything: god, goddess, daimon or djinn, anything that's listening, I ask that Blake or Sinbad are selected to answer the riddle. I'm so unversed in clever things that if our fate rests on my shoulders... I can't even think on it.

A red light appears on the lion's forehead. When it blinks, I assume it's mechanical after all. Another clever, deadly decoy from this Geppetto character. The lion glances at each one of us, and to my horror, finally settles its gaze on me. The red light casts its beam, and a red dot appears on my chest.

"You," it says. "You will answer my riddle. Seek no assistance or you all perish."

I glance at the others, who appear as anxious as I feel. They must have already come to the same conclusion I have—that if this riddle rests on me, we're all doomed. Steeling myself, I wait for the lion's words and try to ignore the frantic pounding of my heart.

When I look at the lion again, it says, "I have cities, but no houses. I have mountains, but no trees. I have water, but no fish. What am I?"

Fuck me! Who comes up with all this nonsense? I rack my brain in despair, but have no bloody idea what the answer could be.

I replay the words repeatedly in my head, hoping that in doing so, the answer will come to me. But, nothing.

Not a damned thing.

Perhaps because my brain has already accepted my fate, my thoughts suddenly turn to Ember. If she were here, she'd come up with the right answer in the blink of an eye. She's the smartest person I've ever met. And when she willingly allowed a clod like me to kiss her, to touch her in her most sacred of places, she became the highlight of my whole life. I can't believe I'm never going to see her again.

The lion doesn't forbid me from moving, so I pace back and forth, turning my brain inside-out for the answer. I know I'm about to fail and death is imminent. The end. But what about Ember? Where is she? Is Blake with her? Are they still alive? I conjure up images of her: riding side-by-side with us on horseback, sleeping in our camp, clinging to the back of the Roc while reciting facts about everything under the sun just so she won't have to pay attention to the dirt staining her person.

I know I'm running out of time.

If this is anything like the other riddles, I don't have long before a horrible fate befalls us. Ember returns to my thoughts as well as the image of her poring over the maps that brought us this far. How lucky I was to be in the company of such a beauty, even for just a little while!

A loud, clattering sound comes from the doors behind the beast. All of our heads jerk up at the sound, but the lion doesn't budge. Why should it? It's waiting for me to answer the riddle—waiting for me to fail. An unexpected roar startles us next, but the roar doesn't come from the lion. It comes from whatever is on the other side of the door.

Ember remains in my thoughts, comforting me during my last moments. I see her decoding the last cipher, her beautiful brow furrowed as the answer to finding the next clue comes to her—

That's it! I think before blurting out, "A map!"

Blake's and Sinbad's heads jerk back with surprise and they look at the lion. The red dot disappears and it rises to its feet, moving closer to me.

"Do you have the map that brought you to this place?" it asks.

Its lifeless gaze penetrates me to the core. It looks so real, but I suspect it's not, at least, not entirely. I suppose there's a chance it's both natural and artificial.

"Well?" it asks again, jarring me from my stupor.

"I do," I say, pulling out the crude map with Ember's notes all over it from my pocket. As I hold it out towards the beast, it grabs the parchment between its teeth and begins to chew it up. Inch by inch, it scarfs the whole map down.

"What in the hells?" Aimes exclaims, but the lion ignores him, content to eat its meal.

I dread what will happen once he finishes. Will he shit out more riddles? Or kill us all? There's no place to hide here. The doors remain closed and the racket coming from behind them makes me grateful they're there in the first place.

This goddamned beast is a very slow eater. More time passes, and my patience grows thin. I even consider taking off its head and hoping for the best. But, then it finishes, and silently walks between us to the doors, where it turns around and sits facing us, as if to watch our next move.

"You are all free to enter," it says and the doors click open behind us, sliding into the walls on either side. None of us needs a second invitation. As soon as the doors open wide enough, we run through them before they can close again.

The clatters and roars I heard earlier are louder now that we're inside the next room. And this next room is filled to the brim with treasure! Any other time, my eyes would have been big as saucers, lapping up the mounds of treasure I see piled all around us. But not now, because my eyes are plastered on what's atop the fortune: Blake and Ember! My heart leaps with relief until I see what's behind them. Something much larger and scalier than Sinbad's Roc.

Oh, what the ever-loving fuck? A dragon? We've entered a fucking dragon's lair?

CHAPTER NINETEEN
EMBER

"No, no, no, no, no," I mutter as Blake and I move cautiously through the treasure room.

The loot is unbelievable, visibly endless in its bounty. Most people would be thrilled to find such a fortune. Yet, it reminds me of my mother's penchant for hoarding, piles of junk collapsing on my head, and my sister, Talia's blank stare. Suddenly, I can't think. Or breathe. My mother's home pales in comparison to this chaotic nightmare.

Still, I must choke down my panic and find the wand. Such a rare magical artifact will be difficult to locate amidst so many riches. After we exhaust the first pile, I nearly succumb to the horrible thought that we'll never find it.

A large head suddenly emerges from the next pile over, sending gold and precious gems arcing across the room in a multi-colored shower. I back away, recalling the roars I heard earlier. The shape of the head and the feathers decorating it make me think it looks like a Roc. At first, I think Sinbad's pet managed to somehow get inside the cave. But this creature is far too large and Sinbad isn't anywhere nearby, so I quickly dismiss that guess. No, it's some other Roc.

The thing caws and shakes its wings free. The debris it scatters causes me to duck as I fear the worst. Then, gathering what courage I have, I look up. I can see its left claw holding the Blue Faerie's wand and I spot the familiar glow coming off the tip. As I watch it, the creature's head morphs into that of a dragon and scales follow suit, covering it entirely. This thing is no Roc.

Jumping to my feet, I grab Blake by the arm and yell, "Run!"

Before he can respond, the creature points the wand at us. A powerful blast from its tip sends us flying through the air. I land on a pile of gold coins and instantly realize we aren't dealing with some mindless beast. This is a shapeshifter, one who has the power to wield the wand without compromising himself.

Blake identifies our foe with a name. "Hassan."

As the creature begins to move toward us, it shapeshifts again. Blake tries to intercept the wand, hoping to snatch it during the transition. But Hassan snaps from his dragon shape into what I assume is his natural form because he now appears like an old, human man. He does so in a matter of seconds. He holds the wand in a threatening manner, aiming it at Blake, who moves defensively in front of me. As though Blake will be able to stop the Blue Faerie's power if Hassan chooses to use it against him.

"I see my reputation precedes me," Hassan replies with a sickening smile. Then he turns the wand my way. "But then, so does yours, sweet Ember Limus. I frequently wondered when and where we might meet.

161

And here you've come to me." He focuses the wand at me. "So thoughtful of you to save me the trouble of hunting you down."

There's only one reason he would know my name. "You know *what* I am?"

"Of course," he replies as though I merely asked him if the sky is blue. "In studying the prophecy and then hearing tales of your extreme mental abilities, I long ago determined you were one of the Chosen. Still, I fully expected to make an inconvenient trip to Sweetland long before now."

"I'm sure she's very sorry to disappoint you," Blake spits, his eyes probing for an opening to exploit.

"Oh, it's far from a disappointment, Your Highness," Hassan corrects him. "Indeed, I consider it a terrible pity. So far as I know, you are the first intruders to make your way past the cave's traps and trickery and here you stand in this exclusive chamber." A subtle change comes to his eyes as he adds, "Now no one will ever learn of your great accomplishment."

"We're not dying here today," I say, pushing past Blake. I can barely even believe my own words. I've never in all my life acted with such courage and bravery and if I actually had the time, I might even feel proud of myself.

"We leave here *with* the wand," Blake adds. "So why don't you save us the trouble by handing it over now?"

Hassan chuckles. "As if you could stop me." He aims the wand behind us and a shockwave of power thunders over our heads. I wonder if he purposely missed us, but then a mountain of treasure falls down over us like an avalanche. I want to scream before it buries me.

My heart pounds against my chest when everything lands on top of me. My bravery evaporates all at once and my anxiety takes over. Once more, I'm in my mother's house, weighed down by heavy collections, struggling to breathe, buried alive under trash. Now, I claw and struggle against the great weight, but to no avail. It won't budge and I can't move!

Despite my fear, I keep pushing until I feel something give just above my head. I emerge from the neck up with a shout when I hear voices yelling nearby. And they're not just any voices, but those of my comrades, my friends! I recognize the sound of Aimes' voice and Vaughn's. They've made it! Hope sparks inside me as a feeling of intense happiness and love well up within me. For a moment I'm stunned by the emotions, but then it dawns on me—I am in love with them, all three of them.

As this realization fires up within me, I feel something else. Another fire deep within my body.

My own power, I tell myself.

Summoning every ounce of strength I can muster, I yell out, "Free me!"

In response, the expensive debris surrounding me explodes, going up and outwards. I keep yelling as my power sizzles through my veins, emptying out into the ether around me. Slowly, the treasure piles swirl around me in grand bursts of color, gradually taking shape. They transform into terraced houses and public buildings, a virtual replica of Sweetland, with me at its center. With a delighted shock, I realize I can organize all the chaos and turn it into perfect order—in this case, a replica of my town.

My pride is quickly demolished when Hassan charges me, running down the freshly cleared "street," and aiming the wand in my direction. My scream fills the room as the neatly piled riches vibrate from my war cry, or rather "war scream." But, then something interesting happens, the shockwave from my voice knocks Hassan off his feet, as if he's just encountered an invisible barrier. The wand slips from his hand, rolling in my direction.

Hassan raises his head and reveals his face, now twisted into a mask of anger, no doubt at being bested by a woman. He scrambles over the floor to recover the wand. I draw in another breath and blast him again, but this time, I'm too late. His fingers wrap around the wand and he turns the thing in my direction, blasting me with a ray of bright blue light. The impact nearly slices me in half. I'm suddenly left feeling open, exposed, and, worst of all, vulnerable.

My body goes icy cold for a moment, and I wonder if Hassan has frozen me. Then I realize I'm now in a different room altogether. The chill fades after I land on a dirty floor. Jumping up, I find I'm imprisoned—dark bars surround me. And, as I take stock of the room, I realize there's nothing other than this gaol, or rather, this cage, in the center of the bright blue room.

"Where am I?" I ask aloud.

The blue color shifts from azure to darkness, as if day instantly surrenders to night. There's dead silence. I ask, "Is anyone here?"

"Oh, yes," a small voice answers from nearby in the darkness. "You're never alone in Wonderland."

A tiny light appears above me, illuminating the inside of my gaol. A fish floats by in the air, winking as it passes. I recoil in shock and fear. What is happening? And how in the world have I ended up in Wonderland? The wand must have the ability to open portals.

A screeching howl rents the air, followed by the laughter of dozens of people in various volumes. I cover my ears. "Stop! Stop right now!"

"Perhaps chaos isn't your strong suit," the voice says as the laughter continues.

"Please, make it stop," I beg again. "Please."

"Alas, I cannot."

The mocking reply angers me and I steady myself, saying, "Then I will." I summon every gram of lung power I have and emit another war scream.

But, nothing happens.

I scream again.

Still, nothing happens.

"Did I forget to inform you that your magic doesn't work here, my lovely?"

"Why not?" I ask, still seeking the source of the voice. "What's blocking it?"

"That'd be the gaol bars. They're reinforced with magic, you know? You're confined along with all the chaos the gaol holds. No limits. No reason. No power."

I'm quiet for a moment as the explanation sinks in. Then a horde of bugs enter my cell, as if from thin air, and arrange themselves in front of me. They're wearing tiny colorful clothing and dancing a little jig. They crawl past me as I let out another scream, without even meaning to.

The subsequent laughter surrounds me, filling my head and overwhelming my senses. My hands shake as my growing anxiety takes over, clouding my thoughts. I can't function with that constant laughter. I can't even think straight!

Despite my increasing trepidation, a few thoughts break through my panic. I recall the voice telling me, *You're never alone in Wonderland.*

Hassan must have sent me here because he knew the consequences of such chaos for someone like me. Eventually, this madness will cause me to become completely insane, myself. Such is the goal of Wonderland—it's the antithesis of order and sense, which I crave and depend on. Lacking anything logical to anchor me, I'll be mercilessly dragged down into the plague of madness. I'll become just like my mother.

"I can't stay here!" I gasp aloud. "Let me out!"

Getting no response, I plead to the electric eel that slaloms through the bars that surround me, "How do I get out of here? What must I do?" It ignores me and continues on its way. It swerves to the adjoining side, making the metal bars sizzle each time it makes contact with them. The last thing to vanish is the bright pink tutu it wears around its middle.

It's hopeless here, I decide, sinking to the floor.

All my gallant bravery was for naught. What little I managed to learn about my power wasn't enough to free me from this awful place and now I'm condemned to lose my mind in this hell, doomed to insanity.

I try to find something to think about that makes logical sense, some rational thought, but the chaos around me continues to grow. Butterflies are now attracted to my cage, whispering words I can't understand. The dancing bugs are forming a line, latching their tiny bodies together while swaying back and forth and making randomly spaced clicking noises.

"I can't stay here," I repeat in a pathetic voice, tears filling my eyes before they float upward. I didn't know Wonderland lacked gravity.

It doesn't lack gravity, I correct myself. *Look at you—you're sitting on the floor.*

Then how?

That's just it—there's no explanation for anything that occurs in Wonderland because Wonderland defies explanation.

From the wretched darkness, a large, striped cat suddenly appears, its mischievous grin beaming across its large face. I watch the creature's body slowly fade away, leaving only its odd smile suspended in the air.

"It's all right, darling," it calmly remarks. "I promise everything will make no sense in no time at all, now that you're one of us."

CHAPTER TWENTY
BLAKE

"Where is Ember?" Vaughn asks, while tossing aside a golden shield he used to block one of Hassan's blasts from the wand. Unfortunately, the mint-condition gold is now partly melted and black, marring its once perfect craftsmanship.

The words barely leave Vaughn's mouth before another blast cuts through the pile of gold coins we're hiding behind, nearly decapitating us. We step sideways to avoid it and swiftly duck as the blast ricochets off the wall behind us. Then we carefully crawl across the floor, looking for another place to hide so we can regroup long enough to launch a counterattack.

"You saw what happened to her just as well as—"

"She's okay," Aimes interrupts as I turn to look at him in question. "I know a teleportation spell when I see one. Hassan hid her somewhere and now we need to find out where."

As far as I'm concerned, whatever Hassan has done to her, his life is now forfeit. If it's the last thing I do, I will make sure he never leaves this cave. That thought steels me long enough to brace for his approach.

To my surprise, Hassan flies forward, but fails to attack. His foot catches on the melted shield, throwing him off balance. As he struggles to right himself, Sinbad sails onto the shapeshifter's back. Hassan tries to aim the wand in his face, but Sinbad drives a knife straight through the middle of his wrist bones. Hassan lets loose a blood-curdling scream as the hand holding the wand snaps open, and it falls sideways into another treasure pile.

Aimes, Vaughn and I spring to our feet immediately, running towards the pile as fast as our legs will carry us. I'm unsure how to retrieve it, since mortals aren't supposed to touch it, but I know we must. If we can manage to separate Hassan from the wand, we stand a much better chance of defeating him.

Speaking of, he and Sinbad are still brawling. Sinbad grabs a silver and gold mace from the floor, using it to club Hassan over the head. The latter stumbles, giving Sinbad an opening, who rushes to the location where the wand disappeared. Meanwhile, the rest of us frantically dig for it, sifting through the riches but to no avail.

A burst of blue suddenly fills the room, signaling the wand's location. It's closest to Sinbad, who immediately sprints for the prize. Unexpectedly, a great snake trips his foot in its jaws, and he face-plants into a pile of jewels. The snake morphs into Hassan, who claws towards the wand.

Vaughn uses his shoulder to ram into the shapeshifter's side. I start running towards the wand while Hassan knocks me aside with a substantial headbutt. Dizzy and trying not to succumb to the sudden stars in my vision, I strike at him with my sword, which he deftly avoids before delivering a hard punch to my face that crosses my eyes.

Hassan is strong, and he's an excellent fighter. Clearly, since he's taking on all three of us.

I turn around and find him grinning triumphantly when a blast of blue light explodes behind him. He lets out a blood-curdling scream before completely vanishing. He just simply blips out of thin air, revealing Sinbad who stands in his place, clinging to the precious wand despite an expression of total agony on his face. Then he simply collapses. The wand slips from his fingers as he clutches his chest.

I run to help him, but I know I'm too late. Leaning down and pressing my ear to his chest confirms my worst suspicion. "He's dead," I sigh.

"Let me see him," Aimes says, pushing me aside. He places his hands on Sinbad's chest only to quickly jerk them away as he faces me with wide eyes. "He's full of the wand's power. I can feel its energy throbbing within him."

"Which means?"

"We can't help him. Not anytime soon, anyway."

"I fear he may not last long," I reply with more concern. I think of the poor Roc waiting for Sinbad outside.

"And I believe you're right," Aimes concurs.

"For now, let's get him out of here," Vaughn barks. "Let's *all* get out of here."

"What of Ember?" Aimes asks.

"We have to find her," I answer, and the others quickly agree.

I wrap the wand with a piece of cloth from my pocket and lay it on Sinbad's chest. It can hardly harm him now. Retrieving a velvet blanket from a nearby mound of coins, we cover him with it, using it as a barrier so we're able to still touch him. We hurry out the doors, hoping desperately to avoid any further traps or obstacles. The long corridor winds upward, but there's no sign of anything dangerous.

We're very watchful as we make our way, in case Hassan returns. Despite the blast Sinbad unloaded on him, shapeshifters are notoriously hard to kill. Hassan could still be somewhere inside the caves. Eventually, we arrive at the cave's entrance, and the other side of the trap door that sucked us down. We step very gingerly around the latter, being careful not to fall into it again. Outside, the Roc remains seated, raising its head at our return.

"Well, thank fuck for that," Vaughn says with obvious relief.

The bird looks at us with disinterest before taking note of the velvet-covered form we carry. A sadness shows on its face as it closes its eyes. It must recognize its master by scent. Opening its eyes, it stands up and spreads its wing downward for us to climb.

"Looks like he's still willing to let us travel on him," Aimes remarks, first to climb on its back.

"Do you know how to fly it?" I ask, draping Sinbad carefully across the creature before climbing up.

"No idea," Aimes replies as Vaughn comes up behind me. "Do either of you?"

"No," I reply.

"Me neither," Vaughn says.

"Guess I'll find out for myself," Aimes responds, grabbing a handful of feathers. Once all of us are aboard, the Roc takes to the skies. Sinbad's body is wedged securely between myself and Vaughn.

"Any idea where we should go?" I call out to Aimes.

As we ponder my question, the dry desert breeze softly blows in our ears. Aimes finally speaks up. "Where would Hassan take her?"

"Someplace where she has no power to retaliate or cause him any more trouble," Vaughn replies.

"Does a place like that even exist?" Aimes asks.

I shake my head just as the answer hits me. "Yes, it does! The same place where things like flying blades and bottomless pits exist… Wonderland!"

"Wonderland?" Vaughn repeats, his eyes narrowing to slits. "Sinbad said those mechanical cats could have come from there."

"It all makes sense now. Plus, it's the most hectic, chaotic and messy place in all of Fantasia—all things that would completely unnerve Ember. Hassan must know Wonderland will break her."

The Roc begins to descend when Aimes's compound comes into sight. I glance at Aimes in surprise.

"Don't look at me," he says and shakes his head. "Maybe the bird knows this is the closest safe haven it could reach in the shortest time."

As we land outside the gates, we dismount and leave Sinbad with his feathered friend—at least, for now. Aimes tucks the wand into his jacket before entering the gates. As he recites the appropriate phrase of the day, we hear the Roc squawk loudly and it spreads its wings. Before we can do anything to stop it, it takes flight, carrying away our remaining supplies and Sinbad with it!

"Dammit!" Vaughn yells, racing after the bird as it soars well above our heads.

Argos emerges from the gates with sadness in his eyes. "It would seem, my brother, that trouble continues to trail your heels."

We spend the next hour telling Argos and the rest of the clan elders what happened in the caves. They listen closely, occasionally nodding with unmasked interest. It breaks my heart to recount this story. All I can think about is Ember. What is she going through and where is she within Wonderland? Every moment I spend here is one less spent to find her.

At the sadness within me and my driving need to go after her, I realize something. I'm in love with Ember and if I were a betting man, I'd say the same goes for Vaughn and Aimes. There's something about her that just fits with the three of us—she's like the fourth wheel to our carriage and now that she's missing, I realize I never want to lose sight of her again.

I love her, and I want to make her mine. Forever.

Argos rises to his feet.

"Have no fear, Aimes," he says. "We have swift horses that will deliver you to Wonderland within a week."

"What about the Roc?" Vaughn asks.

"And Sinbad?" Aimes adds.

"Their path is no longer your own," an elder says.

"Indeed," Argos affirms. "The two are connected by their souls. Even in death, they belong to one another. Thus, the Roc will carry Sinbad home to his own clan."

"I'm not sure if the bird knows where they are," I say, imagining all the people who will mourn Sinbad's passing. "Hassan has taken them captive."

"It matters not," the elder replies calmly. "With Hassan's disappearance, the Roc shall find them in due time. No power exists to prevent such from happening."

"I'm not sure Hassan would agree," Vaughn replies.

"Be that as it may," Argos explains, "I can assure you Hassan no longer wields any power over Sinbad, nor his people after such a defeat. Besides, the Rocs are loyal servants to their masters, even in death. It's why we don't allow such beasts inside our encampment. A single one could destroy us all."

"Yes, we're familiar with the threat," I say, fondly recalling our initial encounter with Sinbad.

174

"But let us waste no more time with idle talk," Argos says. "We shall supply you with provisions and send you on your way. Our sister-in-marriage needs her three husbands!"

CHAPTER TWENTY-ONE
EMBER

I'm clinging to my sanity.

I've been in Wonderland for what seems like a week, judging by my best calculations. But I'm losing my ability to keep count. Every day I feel myself driven closer to the edge. I can feel my intellect slipping away, along with my grip on sanity, because nothing here makes sense.

The moment I think I've wrapped my head around something, it changes. If you aren't already mad when you arrive in Wonderland, you'll get there quickly enough. I do my best to focus on what I've learned about the place in my effort to keep my wits about me. But I fear it's not working.

Here, up is down and down is sideways.

My cell is never empty, and people, animals, and unidentifiables come and go, appearing and disappearing at random. Sometimes they tell me things that make no sense. Other times, they act as if I'm not even there. They sit and have tea parties while speaking in nonsense languages that are purely made up.

And that cat keeps appearing, always fading away slowly into nothing but a smile. 'The Cheshire Cat', they call him. I've heard of him, but he's even more bizarre in person. He's mischievous and infuriating. I just want him to go away, but he won't. He refuses to. Instead, he taunts me and leaves his sarcastic smile behind as a reminder of how crazy I'm becoming. I keep looking for something I can hang onto, anything to hold my mind together, and keep it from splintering into a thousand pieces that may never fit back together again.

The cat constantly repeats a strange poem, called 'The Jabberwocky'. The bizarre words float errantly inside my head, and I pick them out and put them back together again. I measure their style and flow, defining every single word, listing its synonyms and antonyms. I analyze the only thing I can cling to in this place, using the poem like a warm blanket wrapped around my fragile mind.

It's hard to stay positive, but I try. I fight the ceaseless urge to spiral down into despair and resist the lure of the bottomless abyss in the cave of my thoughts. I think of Aimes and Blake and Vaughn. And I think of Sinbad, too, and his great bird. I can't imagine them being any match for Hassan as long as he's in command of the Blue Faerie's wand. If I couldn't shut him down, I doubt they'd do better.

This must be my punishment for being greedy. I fell in love with three men, more than my fair share, so now they must be taken from me. Now I'm doomed for eternity to dwell in the madness of this private hell. Perhaps I should simply end my pain. Grant myself some peace instead of waiting for the madness to snatch away my sense of self forever. I'm not sure what I can really do though, lacking any magic and being without any belongings. But, I'm hopeful I can find a way to end my pain.

I'm jolted back to the present. At least, to what I think is the present. Someone is entering my cell. I look up at her to decide if she's real or not. Her beauty is astounding, unparalleled to any woman I've ever laid eyes on. Her hair is pure ivory, her skin perfect alabaster. Her bright eyes are a gorgeous shade of periwinkle.

I reach out to touch her, eager to confirm whether she's make believe. But she touches me first, placing her hand on my face, and caressing my cheek gently and delicately. A peaceful feeling washes over me, a calm like I've never known.

"My name is Harmonia," she whispers before kissing the hollow space between my ear and neck. I feel her touch tingle there. "My kiss is a magical brand. It allows my power to help you stay at peace." She pulls back with dread. "But it won't last forever. It's only temporary until you can find the peace you need for yourself." She takes a couple steps back. "Now, leave this place."

"I can't," I protest. "Hassan sealed me in this cage. I can't get out."

"Yes, you can," she says, as though the answer should already be obvious. "You just need someone to replace you."

"Replace me?" I repeat. "Even if I knew someone who would take my place, I'm powerless to bring them here."

Harmonia hums. "Maybe you don't *have* to bring them here. Perhaps they're already present."

Being trapped in this cell hasn't deprived me of all my wits. "You mean you?" She nods. "Why would you willingly imprison yourself here?"

"That's not your worry," Harmonia says with a wagging finger. "This gaol is designed to house only one occupant after it's activated. There are now two of us, so one of us can leave. I'll remain ,so you may go."

"No," I say, my sense of justice rising to the fore. "I can't let you do—"

My words are cut off and the familiar sensation of a chill runs deep inside my bones…

I suddenly find myself on a patch of grass outside.

Odd-looking flowers surround me in bizarre shapes and brilliant colors. A white rabbit in a bowtie hops by, followed closely by a frog who glances at me through his monocle before standing on his hind legs and walking away, remarking on the weather. The madness here isn't much of an improvement over that in the cell.

Taking a quick look around, I spot a trail that glows in rainbow hues. No doubt the power given to me by Harmonia helps steer me in the right direction. I don't have a better choice, so I follow it.

I hope it's the way out of Wonderland.

I walk on a checkered path and suddenly hear the sound of approaching footfalls—marching in a regular rhythm. I stand still on the path, mesmerized by the perfect clicking pattern the numerous heels make against the tiles. When those making the commotion come into view, I realize I shouldn't have remained because they appear to be soldiers.

I scurry off the path, throwing myself into a large patch of mushrooms bigger than I am. I hide behind the stem of one of the immense mushrooms, peeking around one side. I almost scream when a voice speaks to me from above. "What are you doing?"

I look up to find a pink and green, striped beetle. It looks down at me, where I stand beneath the mushroom cap, its beady, black eyes glaring at me.

"I'm… hiding."

"From the Red Queen's guard?" It asks as I nod, figuring the 'Red Queen's Guard' must be the title for the soldiers I just witnessed.

"Why?" the creature asks. "Are they looking for you?"

"No, but I don't want them to *start* looking for me."

"A sound policy when it comes to she who lops off heads. What is your name?"

"Ember."

The beetle gives its unique version of a bow. "Sheffield B. Hornsbury, Esquire at your service. Do you suppose the guards might be looking for me, too?"

"I don't know."

"And I have no wish to find out. We should therefore evacuate the premises post haste. Do you know the way?"

"No, I was looking for a way out when I ran right into the guards."

"And they're the absolute worst," he says, nodding. "Not that the other guards fail to live down their unpleasant reputations."

Not wanting to get side-tracked, I say, "I wish I knew which way to go."

"Oh, I know the way."

"Then why haven't you already left?"

He motions to his back where one of his wings is broken.

"My problem is one of a lack of locomotion. Can I solve that by riding upon your shoulder?"

I offer my right shoulder to him. "You certainly can."

Sheffield climbs down the stem of the mushroom and sits on my shoulder. He quietly waits until the last of the Red Queen's Guard marches by. I peek around the mushroom once more to make sure they're well out of sight and earshot.

"Ah, very good," Sheffield says. "Now turn around."

"Turn around?'

"Yes. The way out is in the opposite direction."

I follow his directions as we make our way across a field of purple strawberries. Then we trudge through a thicket of weaving, bobbing bushes with bright colors that blend and change with each movement. Emerging, we encounter a blonde woman wearing garb associated with a huntress. She zeroes in on me and raises her bow.

"Is she going to shoot us?" Sheffield asks in a high-pitched voice.

"Looks like," I say as I attempt to hide behind a tree. The tree shrieks and jumps sideways, leaving us exposed.

Sheffield screams when the huntress lets loose an arrow that soars toward my face. He jumps free, yelling at me as he latches onto one of the other trees. I dart to one side, but an arrow sizzles through the air and strikes my arm, continuing forward even as it leaves a deep gash that burns like the nine hells.

"I'm just going to stay right here," Sheffield announces before skittering further upward to hide among the leaves. "If you don't get killed, you'll want to follow the river. It'll take you away from here."

Grabbing my wounded arm, I make a run through the moving trees, begging them to help me. All they do is part and make me an easy target as the huntress closes in behind me. When the river comes into view, I remember I can use my powers, which hopefully will work this time. Just as the huntress pulls back her bow, I emit a loud and high-pitched scream, saying, "Stop!"

The arrow stops dead in its arc before falling to the ground as if the huntress had merely dropped it. That distracts her long enough for me to reach the river and I waste no time in running along the side of it. All the while, I pray I'm indeed headed in the right direction.

CHAPTER TWENTY-TWO
BLAKE

Wonderland is brimming with illogical creatures, but the sights keep surprising me. I glance nervously at the river beside us, just in case the waters decide to make similar mischief. Aimes claims the river is the sole thread of sanity in this insane land, but I dare take no chances. Only the thought of Ember keeps me going and I know the same is true for both Aimes and Vaughn.

We've gone just a little further when something catches my eye in the distance—a woman. I hone in on her and before my brain can label my eyes as deceptive, I realize the woman is Ember! She's running, stumbling as she anxiously glances behind her. When she comes closer, I can see blood pouring from her arm, staining one side of her blouse. An arrow, meanwhile, flies over her shoulder, narrowly missing her head.

"Dammit, someone's after her," Vaughn yells, pulling his weapon free.

"Pincer formation!" I shout, pulling my own weapon loose. "Hurry!" I dig my heels hard into the horse's flanks while Aimes and Vaughn split off to either side. I head straight toward Ember at a full gallop.

Please, gods and goddesses, let me make it in time.

"Blake!" she screeches in a deep rasp. "She's trying to kill me!"

Her words come out in short gasps. I rein my horse as she lurches towards it. As I reach down to grab her, my hand slips on the bloody slickness from her arm, but I manage to lift her into the saddle behind me.

I watch as Vaughn and Aimes go after the huntress who was trying to kill her. They successfully chase her away from the two of us.

As soon as Ember's seated, she screams. As I turn around, I realize another patch of blood is beginning to flow from just below her collarbone, on the other side. Just the very tip of the arrow still sticks out of the wound.

"Is it bad?" she whispers.

"I don't know," I tell her. "We'll get you help."

"Dammit, the bitch got away," Vaughn calls out as he and Aimes return, their horses gasping for breath. Obviously, the huntress gave them a good chase.

"Should we go after—" The question dies in Vaughn's throat when he looks down at the blood covering Ember's clothes. His face twists into a mask of anger and he wheels his horse around.

"No, let the huntress go," I say, snagging his arm. "Ember needs us." Vaughn gives the huntress a defiant grunt before turning around and, together with Aimes and me, gallops to the Wonderland border.

I turn and look down at Ember as she slouches against my back. Though she's bleeding badly from the second arrow, I don't dare remove it without proper supplies to manage the what will turn out to be even more blood. I only hope the missile isn't dipped in poison.

Despite her injuries, Ember seems surprisingly composed. Once, the sight of blood alone would have been enough to put her on edge. But now, she seems oblivious to it.

"I know a healer at the edge of Ascor," Aimes says, keeping a worried eye on our shared wife. "The river will take us straight to him."

"Where... where's Sinbad?" Ember asks.

I look down at her grimly, wishing she hadn't asked the question. "He didn't make it."

"He didn't make it?" she repeats, becoming more alert all of a sudden.

"He had to use the Blue Faerie's wand against Hassan," I explain.

"Sinbad saved us even though doing so destroyed him in the process," Aimes explains and his eyes are downcast. We all feel the loss of our newest friend. "His Roc took him home to his people."

"The beast took him?" Ember asks.

"We tried to stop the bird but it was no good," Vaughn grumbles.

"Argos was certain that nothing could keep the Roc from reuniting both of them with Sinbad's clan," Aimes concludes, turning his horse slowly.

"Some comfort, I suppose," she says. "Still..." She shakes herself awake and I can hear tears in her voice when she says, "He will be... very much missed. It's so unfair."

"Life so often is," I reply and then decide to change the subject because I want her to focus on happier occasions. "How did you manage to escape?"

"This woman…" she starts and then grows quiet as if she isn't sure of her own words.

"A woman?"

"Yes… she took my place in the gaol. She called herself Harmonia."

The name sends shivers down my spine. "Harmonia?" I repeat and Ember nods.

"You mean Discordia?" Vaughn asks, his eyes as narrowed as mine. Aimes, too, for that matter. All three of us know Discordia is no friend.

"Discordia?" Ember repeats. "I… I don't know what you mean, Blake."

"We'll talk about it later," I reply as the trees finally cease their movements. "Right now, the only subject we need to focus on is getting you to the healer."

We swiftly ride across a short expanse of desert and reach the edge of Ascor. Ember seems to grow weaker with each mile. The blood loss and difficulty from riding horseback with an arrow stuck in her are taking their toll.

When we reach the hut, we swiftly dismount and I carry her inside, immediately noting the man who walks up to meet me at his front door.

"What's happened to the young miss then, hmm?" the healer asks as soon as we enter the hovel. He glances at Ember who, by now, is barely conscious, and babbling about her mother and sister as she drifts in and out of lucidity.

The healer, an old and hunched over man with long scraggly gray hair and an equally scraggly and gray beard, motions for me to carry Ember to a long and narrow wooden table in the center of the room. I do as instructed and he bends over her, inspecting her as well as her wounds. Without saying a word, he reaches out and clips the feathered end of the arrow before pulling it free, making Ember gasp loudly. He shushes her as if he's talking to a baby and then immediately turns to a tankard behind him, fetching it and then pouring the liquid within over her wounds.

"What is that?" Vaughn demands.

"Liquor," the healer answers. Ember, meanwhile, moans out her pain while the old man staunches the flow of blood with thick pads of cotton. He replaces them several times before the bleeding stops. Cutting the material of her shirt away from the wound, he examines the injury more closely.

"Good, it's a clean wound," he sighs with relief. "The arrow didn't hit anything vital, either. I can fix that right up."

"Well, be quick about it," Vaughn growls, his concern fastened on Ember.

"It takes as long as it takes." He gestures towards the door. "Now, will you all kindly step outside?"

"No," Aimes says.

"Not happening," Vaughn adds.

"Fine, then *one* of you can stay, but this place is much too small for all three of you and I don't appreciate tight quarters while I'm tending to the wounded!"

The old man nods toward me. "You can stay. But you two…" He indicates the door with his thumb.

"Do as he asks," I tell them and they promptly obey.

Once they close the door behind them, I watch the man grind up a few powders with what appear to be herbs in a bowl with a pestle. He adds a few drops of this and then pushes half the mixture into the sizable gash where the arrow entered her body. With her wound treated, he smears a bit of the leftover paste onto her arm, which is barely grazed.

"That should do it," he says.

I look back at him. "How long will it take for her to heal?"

He glances at me with obvious annoyance. "Are you as deaf as your man is?"

"No, and my fist is much closer to you," I tell him in an impatient voice. "How long?"

"Hard to say," the healer admits. "The wound's clean, but she's lost a bit of blood. The mixture should help."

"How will we know when it works?"

"She'll open her eyes and get off the table."

"It will be awhile then?"

"Yes. Cup of tea?"

"Might as well."

"Your men would like one too?"

"They're more interested in harder beverages."

"There's a pub a short way down the river."

When I lean out the door to tell them, neither one makes any motion to leave. I know I wouldn't if I were in their place, either.

I'm still sipping my tea when Ember opens her eyes and turns her head to look at me quizzically. She's been unconscious for hours. Taking a deep breath, she sits up and continues to look at me from the table top, asking where she is.

"You're safe," I respond as I get up and walking over to her, take her into my arms. I'm careful not to disrupt her bandages.

"How do you feel?" the healer asks, making sure she's steady as I bring her to rest on her feet.

"I feel... okay," she answers, then shakes her head. "But, I'm confused as to how I came to be here in the first place. I don't... I can't remember what happened."

"A huntress in Wonderland shot you with a couple of arrows," I tell her, then I motion to the old man in front of her. "He saved your life."

"Thank you," she replies, still scanning her soiled garments and healing skin.

I note the thick scars already forming where her wounds were, even though her pale skin regains some of its natural color. I wonder how she'll handle having such telltale marks on her once-flawless skin,

189

considering how she insists on everything being so perfect and pristine all the time. I avert my eyes before she notices me inspecting her. I don't want her to feel more self-conscious than I know she already does. Even with the marks, she remains perfect in my mind.

"Time for my payment," the healer says, wiggling his fingers. I drop a small pouch into his hands before taking Ember's arm and escorting her to the door. When I open it, Vaughn and Aimes all but run to her.

"I didn't expect you to be up so soon," Vaughn marvels.

"I did," Aimes says with a smile before leaning over to kiss her on the cheek.

"Are you okay?" Vaughn asks.

She nods and allows him to hold her for a moment or two before she pulls away and faces Aimes.

"Can you clean me?" she whispers almost desperately.

"There's a pub further down the river," Vaughn says as he faces Ember. "While we order food, Aimes can take you to the privy and fix you up."

CHAPTER TWENTY-THREE
AIMES

Now within the privacy of the privy inside the tavern, I look down at Ember, reading her aura in order to ascertain how well she is. She appears to be on the mend. Reaching out for her hand, she gives it to me willingly and I begin to cleanse all the dirt and dust from her person.

"Aimes," she says and then hesitates.

"Yes?"

"I want…" her voice fades again and a blush steals across her cheeks. She looks up at me and smiles as I give her the time she needs to say whatever is on her mind.

"I want you to show me what physical love is between a man and a woman."

"Right now?" I ask, unable to shake the surprise from my tone.

She nods and smiles up at me shyly.

"But the others are," I start but she interrupts me with a shake of her head.

"Just you and me," she says.

I suddenly want to be inside her immediately and she's thankfully more than ready to accommodate the ache I have for her. As I watch, she unbuttons her trousers and allows them to pool at her feet. Then she guides my hand to the valley between her legs and such is all the encouragement I need.

By the time I touch her, she's already soaking wet. And realizing time is of the essence, I decide not to give time to foreplay. She's ready for me. Thus, I drop my own trousers and release my full and hearty cock, which springs to attention immediately. She looks down at it and her eyes widen with surprise.

"I…" she starts and then swallows hard. "Will the whole thing fit?"

I chuckle. "Every last inch."

I envelop her waist within my hands and lift her, instructing her to spread her legs to accommodate my hips. Then I push her up against the wood-planked wall and she wraps her legs around my waist. My cock is poised at her entrance, but I don't push into her just yet.

"My dear, this will hurt, but the pain will be quick."

"I don't care," she breathes as she looks up at me and then nudges her pelvis forward as if to encourage me. I push forward and the head of my cock stretches her. Immediately, she throws her head back and gasps. The gasp is quickly followed by a moan.

As I push into her, I enjoy the way my erection divides her, filling her as if we were custom-fitted by a master toolmaker. She is incredibly tight and yet also slick with her own need.

It's my turn to gasp as I slip past her maidenhead and fully seat myself inside her hot, dripping center. She inhales a pinched sound as I break past her barrier, but moments later, she begins moaning loudly.

I grind my hips forward, sinking myself fully into her tight orifice as she lets out another loud moan of pleasure. I alternate between fucking her slowly (and enjoying her coos) and slamming myself into her (making her grunt and scream). I wrap my hand around her neck without applying any pressure, just letting it rest there. I like the way her voice vibrates against my palm.

She bites her lip when I push fully inside her and a moment later, pull her upward, placing my hands on her waist again and sliding her up and down the length of my hard cock.

She coos as I fill her with my sex, pushing apart her slick folds with the most delicious friction until I can no longer restrain myself. At that moment, nothing exists beyond the two of us, making our connection much more gratifying than just physical. I shudder as her body surrenders to mine, shattering into a thousand small pieces when her orgasm explodes through her.

Her breasts are covered with perspiration and I grind down into her even harder, eager to please her the same way she pleases me. Tilting her hips forward, I push into more deeply, hearing the low growl of bliss rising from my throat as I release my own orgasm—a climactic flood inside her.

###

Now inside the pub proper, Ember and I find the others seated at a table near the back. It's out of the way and mostly private, giving us a chance to talk.

"Took you long enough," Vaughn says.

Ember immediately smiles and glances down, a blush stealing over her cheeks as I look at her and she looks at me and we both laugh.

"Just what were you doing in there?" Blake asks.

"Mind your business," Ember responds, giving him a flirtatious smile that makes him smile in turn.

Soon, the food and ale arrive and everyone heartily digs in.

After a few minutes, Ember takes a deep breath and asks, "What shall we do about Sinbad?"

"What do you mean?" Blake asks.

"The Roc took him home," Vaughn supplies.

"I mean to avenge him," she explains, her eyes going hard.

"We can discuss that topic when there aren't so many ears around," Vaughn cautions.

I nod my agreement. "For now, let's get some food in our bellies and find somewhere safe for a night's sleep. We've a long ride back to Sweetland."

After we devour our food and beers, we head towards a place Vaughn knows of between Ascor and the Forest of No Return, where we hunker down for the night. While Vaughn takes first watch, Ember is cradled safely between Blake and me. She tells us about her adventures in Wonderland.

"I honestly didn't know what was real and what wasn't until Harmonia appeared," she says at the end of her narrative.

"But why would she help you?" Blake asks as he lies behind her. "She's a monster."

"She definitely wasn't a monster as far as I could tell," Ember argues. "She was kind and she was the only one who was. After all, she gave up her freedom so I could leave."

Blake appears worried. "Then you really don't know who she is?"

She looks over her shoulder at him and shakes her head. "Should I?"

"Have you never heard of Discordia?" I ask.

"Well, yes. She was a dreadful monster, but what does she have to do with Harmonia?"

"Ember," Blake says patiently, "as hard as this is to grasp, Harmonia *is* Discordia. They're one and the same."

"That's not possible," Ember argues. "How could the woman who freed me from that prison be the same person who turns people into zombies, and even worse?"

"I don't know how," I reply slowly. "But it's true."

"I'd heard that she changed not so long ago," Vaughn interrupts from the door. The first watch must have ended. "Maybe she reverted back to the good person she used to be," he surmises as he takes Blake's place.

Ember squints. "Reverted?"

"She wasn't always evil," I explain. "She was turned into Discordia."

Ember nods. "Maybe she's trying to make up for all the harm she's done."

"I suppose anything's possible," I reply. "Anyway, she'll not be doing too much harm from a Wonderland gaol."

Blake sighs. "Better get on watch." He looks down at Ember fondly. "Good night." She says the same before leaning up to kiss him. That ends with all of us kissing her before Vaughn cuddles up closer to her. He's asleep in seconds while I pull her into my arms.

I keep my arms wrapped around her, holding her close but gently. "I'm so glad you're back," I whisper as I nuzzle her ear.

"Me too," she whispers. "I was so… scared in Wonderland."

"So was I. And Blake too," I answer on a sigh, remembering the awful place. "And it was the first time I ever saw true fear on Vaughn's face." When I see how distraught Ember starts to become, tears welling in her eyes, I add, "I'm sorry we failed to protect you."

"There was nothing any of you could have done," she answers, shaking her head as I clean the tears from her cheeks. "I wish I could have done something for Sinbad," she continues on a whisper. "I have so much to learn about my power."

"In time, everything will begin to make sense to you," I respond.

CHAPTER TWENTY-THREE
BLAKE

When Aimes and Vaughn fall asleep, I approach Ember because I can tell she isn't yet asleep.

"Can we talk?" I ask.

She nods as she sits up and a subject that's been on my mind for days now comes to the fore. I clear my throat. "When we finally get to the other side of all of this chaos of war and battle, I want to spend the rest of my forever with you, Ember."

She turns to face me, her delicate fingers caressing my face. "I would like that."

But, I'm not sure she understands what I'm saying. "I mean... I want to marry you."

"We're already married, remember?" she asks on a laugh.

But, I shake my head. "That was according to Aimes's clan. I mean... I want to marry you in front of the eyes of Sweetland and all of Fantasia."

She's quiet for a moment and worries her lower lip, and I wonder if I've misjudged her feelings for me. Then I wonder if perhaps she's never gotten past the fact that I forced her into this journey, using her family as collateral.

"What about Aimes and Vaughn?" she asks. "It's been... the four of us all along."

"I didn't mean that we would exempt them from our nuptials," I answer on a laugh. "I believe all four of us should be together."

"We can… we can do that?"

I chuckle again. "When you're a royal, you make your own rules. Have as many lovers as you please."

She giggles. "You three are plenty."

I nod, for I'm content to hear as much. I can't imagine the fact that she'd need more than three men, but what do I really know? When the silence between us becomes pervasive, I bring up another subject about which I'm curious. "Did you and Aimes," I start.

She nods almost guiltily as her eyes widen. "I hope that doesn't… bother you."

I shake my head even though it does bother me slightly—only because I wasn't the first of us to have her. "No, I understand why you chose him to be your first." Then I clear my throat. "Did… did you enjoy it?"

She nods. "It was… quite incredible."

"Will you tell me about it?"

She nods again and carefully separates herself from the sleeping Aimes and Vaughn. I help her to her feet and she collapses into my arms as we share an extremely passionate kiss. Then she proceeds to explain how Aimes fucked her and, from the sound of it, did quite a good job. Of course, my own cock hardens at the retelling and I reach down to stroke it above my pants.

"Are you too sore for round two?" I ask as she stares at my length, which strains the fabric of my trousers.

"No," she answers and immediately pulls away from me, removing her pants as I stare at the valley between her thighs. At the thought that I can finally bury my cock within her, I'm almost ecstatic.

"I'm not... in a slow and soft mood," I warn her. "Your story about Aimes stoked the fires of my jealousy, I'm afraid." She doesn't say anything, but her eyes go a bit wider. "Take my cock out, Ember."

She nods and swallows hard as she fusses with my trousers until she releases my cock and it eagerly jumps forth. I reach for her hand and taking it, wrap it around my girth, teaching her how to stroke me up and down.

"Now get on your knees."

She does as I tell her as she swallows hard and, taking a handful of the hair at the nape of her neck, I hold her head in place as I thrust my erection between her lips. Her eyes go wider as she looks up at me, and the shock within her expression makes me only want to shove myself into her even deeper.

It's takes all I've got to resist the urge to blast my stream into her sweet mouth the moment I feel the back of her throat. Despite my stamina, it's been a while since I've been buried inside a woman. Even longer since I've been inside a woman's mouth this way. And it feels like heaven. Ember wraps her lips around my cock like a sleeve, sucking and licking me.

It's a beautiful thing as I watch her take every inch of me down that gorgeous throat. But, it's not long before I want to feel her other lips wrapped around me. Pulling myself free from her mouth, I help her to her feet and then turn her around, bending her over. Then I slide the head of my engorged manhood against her tight and wet opening as I tease her.

At the thought that Aimes filled her only moments earlier, I want her all the more.

"Please," she whimpers as she tries to back against me.

I thrust within her in one fluid moment and she yelps as I slam into her core, burying myself up to my stomach. She's tighter than I remember another woman ever being. With my other hand, I reach between her thighs and begin rubbing her clit as I pull my cock out and shove inside her again.

"Tell me again what Aimes did to you," I order her and as she says the words between gasps and moans of pleasure, I fuck her in long, deep strokes.

When she finishes her story, she succumbs to her own orgasm and begins shaking as it captures her. I hold her in place because I'm not finished with her. Not yet.

"Tell me you will be my wife," I whisper. She doesn't answer right away, so I slam into her even harder with my cock. She gasps as I repeat my question.

"I will be wife… to all three of you," she manages finally.

"Yes," I whisper into her ear as I grind side to side, my cock seated within her fully. "And I will watch Vaugh fuck you and I'll watch Aimes fuck you."

"Oh, yes," she moans.

"And you'll take us all at the same time."

She nods as, at the thought, I pull out of her and release myself all over her back.

When Aimes wakes me for the third watch in the early hours of the morning, I tell him about my rather untraditional proposal to Ember. He seems as pleased about it as Vaughn is. I'm sure either man would have preferred to be the official husband to our beautiful woman, but they don't seem opposed to sharing her.

The dawn breaks, and I'm alarmed to see something large moving nearby behind a copse of thick bushes and trees. I quickly wake the others, prepared to do battle with whatever might attempt to take us on. But, as the creature comes closer, we all stare in amazement at the familiar Roc, which rises into the air before settling down in front of us.

"Is that…" Ember begins, her voice trailing away.

"Yes," I answer. "Looks like Sinbad made it back to his clan, after all."

The bird caws as it lowers its wing towards us, and I wave in response.

"Aimes, Vaughn, let's unpack the supplies from the horses. Now we've got a better mode of traveling."

Aimes asks, "We're going to just leave the horses out here?"

"There are many homesteads in this area and their owners will be very pleased to take in such well bodied beasts," I assure him. "Besides, we'll make much faster headway on that great beast of a bird."

CHAPTER TWENTY-FOUR
AIMES

"So, what do you think?" I ask, standing back for Ember to get a better look at herself in the mirror.

"It's... It's just incredible," she says breathlessly, twisting back and forth to get a better look at the wedding gown I made for her, or that *my magic* made for her.

It sparkles as the light hits the thousands of tiny precious gems that create the entire gown. The fit is flawless perfection, the jewels carefully arranged to caress every curve of her body. The hourglass shape supports her lovely breasts, pushing them up to swell slightly above the corseted top. The bodice highlights her tiny waist before flaring outward into a full skirt. Satin gloves on either arm and a smooth lining protect her delicate skin from the sharp facets.

I watch her swishing about, smiling broadly in the mirror. She remains the most beautiful woman I've ever laid eyes on.

A pang of distress crosses her face as she looks down at her bare feet. "Oh, no! I don't have any shoes to wear with such a beautiful dress."

"Oh, yes, you do," I tell her, turning around to retrieve the small shoe box. I pull a glass slipper free and hold it out toward her.

"That's breathtaking!" she gushes. "Where did you find it?"

"Same place I *found* your dress."

"Where?"

"I made it."

"But how?"

"A bit of water, a bit of fire, a bit of sand, and a bit of magic."

She smiles at me again, putting forth a single foot to try the slipper on. After admiring it, I slip it onto her small foot, followed by the other. In moments, she begins dancing around, clicking and clacking along the tiled floor before coming back to grab my hands in hers.

"Dance with me, Aimes," she giggles. "I've never seen such an incredible dress in my life!"

I kiss her on the cheek, and we dance around the room. "You're absolutely stunning."

Vaughn appears in the doorway, making a clucking sound with his tongue. "I don't think you're supposed to be dancing with the bride before the wedding," he laughs.

"Oh, come join us," Ember says with a coy giggle.

"No, thanks. Dancing isn't really my thing. In fact, I was sent to retrieve you for the ceremony."

"But I'm not ready yet!" she exclaims, sounding anxious again as she turns to me. "I still have to attend to my hair and my face! Goodness, a girl can't get married without any rouge!"

"Oh, I took care of all of that while we were dancing," I assure her with a grin.

She whirls around and looks in the mirror. Her eyes widen when she takes in the curls pinned atop her head and the cascading waterfall of hair that splashes down her back, not to mention her ruby red lips and stained cheeks.

"Thank you!" she gushes. She kisses me softly on the cheek before running toward Vaughn and kissing him, as well. "I'm so excited!"

The two of us walk her out of the room and down the hallway. Soon enough, we're standing before the double doors that lead to the grand ballroom where the ceremony is scheduled to take place. Ember preferred to skip all the pomp and fanfare, but a prince must have a royal wedding. Judging by how everyone is sneaking glimpses of her every chance they get, they must be eager to see Blake wed the lovely Ember. Little do they know such won't be the end of the ceremony, as there are actually three grooms, not one.

"Your Highness," I say as I place Ember's hand in Blake's before taking my place beside them. I'm now officially the newly appointed royal advisor. Vaughn joins me as the highest ranking general ever appointed to the crown service. He outranks all others in the kingdom.

My heart nearly bursts when I see how stunning Ember looks in the special wedding ensemble I created just for her. How happy she is when she and Blake exchange their vows in front of so many friends, family, and important visitors. They're all smiles when they kiss for the first time as husband and wife, and then it's my turn.

The audience seems slightly shocked when I take Blake's place, and he steps aside. But, as he's the prince, no one dares say a word against him or this proceeding, so I marry Ember before the assembled crowd and Vaughn is next. Then the four of us make our way down the aisle, cheered on by the masses seated on either side of us, though they do still seem to be somewhat amazed and taken off guard.

As to the four of us? We just laugh at their disbelief.

Afterwards we attend the grand party and feast. Plenty of wine and sources of merriment abound, as are typically associated with wedding receptions, but on a much grander scale since Blake is the prince.

Blake and Ember share the first dance, waltzing across the checkered tiles to a tender melody, the light from the numerous chandeliers catching the crystal of Ember's gown. Soon the ditty is over and the two break apart as the music picks up. Ember turns around and, spotting Vaughn and me, hurries towards us, immediately grabbing Vaughn's hand and forcing him onto the floor even though he protests.

I can't help but laugh. How awkward Vaughn dances with her… at first. But, Vaughn is always full of surprises, and dances quite well once he overcomes his own self-consciousness. The song finishes and Ember immediately heads for me. I'm happy to accompany her and together, we walk to the center of the floor and begin swaying back and forth to an upbeat melody until the music slows again. Then I pull her close.

"When this party is over, I'll need your help to get out of this dress without damaging it," she purrs.

"It would be my pleasure and privilege, Your Highness."

"And you can tell me all about your council meetings."

"Really? You'd like to hear about them?"

"Of course, really."

"They're rather dry and boring and don't make for stimulating pillow talk on your wedding night."

"That's where you're wrong," she says as I twirl her and she smiles up at me. "You, of all people, should know how I love dry, boring details."

"Very well then," I reply when the music stops and people all around us applaud.

We step off the dance floor and make our way towards Blake, who's talking to a few dignitaries. Ember suddenly pulls me behind a curtain hanging in front of one of the walls and kisses me fiercely.

"I love you, Ember," I tell her when the kiss ends. "And I always will."

"And I will always love you," she says, caressing my cheek before a naughty expression crosses her face. "What do you say to helping me release myself from this gown while also releasing yourself from the constrictions of your own clothes?"

"Why, Your Highness, are you propositioning me?"

"I most certainly am," she teases. "And if I understand your place in the royal court, you're hardly in any position to refuse."

"Then your wish is my command."

The two of us slip down the hallway behind the curtains. We make our way to her bedroom chamber, where I carefully remove her dress using just a bit of magic. Standing in front of me in her wedding lingerie, I feel myself instantly harden. I watch her slip off her brassiere and panties before she lies across the bed. The only thing she's still wearing are her stockings and the glass slippers I made for her. I reach to remove them, but she stops me.

"Leave them on," she coos, stretching her legs upward. She casts an uneasy eye towards the door. "But hurry. We don't have much time before they notice we're missing."

"Let them wait," I reply before burying my face in her sweet center, pleasuring her until she digs her nails into my back and moans happily. I give her what she wants, including several orgasms before stepping back to position myself on the bed. I run my hands up the backs of her legs, spreading them apart and placing each calf over my shoulders before entering her with one smooth stroke. I begin fucking her in long, fluid thrusts as she moans beneath me.

"I could spend the whole night inside you," I whisper.

"Mmm," she murmurs, lost to the moment we make love, at first slowly but picking up our pace, due to the urgency of the possibility of being caught.

She bites her lip to quell her moans of pleasure while clutching the bed linens on either side of her, bracing herself as best she can. I hold her ankles above my shoulders, giving her everything I have to offer. She lets out a long moan and her body convulses in a wave of orgasmic bliss just as I experience my own climax, filling her up until she's dripping with my seed.

Spreading her legs further apart, she bends her knees, allowing me to move downward to kiss her. We intertwine both our bodies and tongues for a few moments before I pull out once again. I offer her my hand and help her to her feet. Then I clean her and magically adjust her hair, slightly disheveled from our tryst.

Helping her slip into a fresh gown, one more suitable for a reception than a wedding, I allow her to exit alone. Then I emerge after I'm certain any prying eyes have departed the scene.

Walking back into the ballroom, Ember stands beside Blake, talking freely with the guests. Blake catches my eye and smiles, shaking his head as if to tell me he knows what we were just up to. I smile in return before snatching a drink from one of the trays being passed around.

CHAPTER TWENTY-THREE
VAUGHN

"I have to go," I tell Blake and Ember after most of the wedding guests leave. "I've just gotten word that Tinker's waiting for me at Bloodstone Castle."

"What? You can't just leave," Ember protests, shaking her head as her mouth drops open. "The party isn't over and it's our wedding night!"

"I'm afraid I don't have a choice. Tinker's already waiting for me with Maura LeChance and the Blue Faerie. I need to get the wand to them quickly."

"It can't wait just one more night?"

I look at her with real regret. "I wish it could, Ember."

"I know this is important," she says, her expression thoughtful. "When you see them, I want you to ask them something for me."

Ember tells me what's on her mind and I nod. Blake agrees with her and we say our goodbyes. I kiss her on the cheek, much more politely than I want to. But others are watching and I'll be back soon enough to make up for my absence.

Heading to the Roc, I climb aboard the beast and direct it to Bloodstone Castle. In Sinbad's absence, I've adopted the bird as my own. That is, if anyone can really own a Roc.

###

When we land at Bloodstone Castle, I'm not surprised to see a large, green-tinted man standing outside the doors to the Blue Faerie's cottage. He watches me with wary eyes as I approach, looking me up and down for a moment.

"Been a long time, Vaughn," he finally says.

"That it has," I concur. "How have you been?"

"Busy."

I clear my throat. "Is the Blue Faerie expecting me?"

"Aye. She's with Maura and Tinker."

"Good. I've got to return to Sweetland as soon as I can."

"Trouble?"

"Only the good kind."

My old friend smiles. "A woman then."

"*The* woman. The only one that will ever matter to me."

"Never figured you as the type to settle down."

"Who said anything about settling down?" I answer on a chuckle.

He simply shakes his head as he escorts me inside the cottage. As soon as I enter, the Blue Faerie looks up and me and I see relief in her eyes.

"Do you have it?" she asks. Beside her are Maura and Tinker.

"I do," I respond, pulling the wrapped cloth from my jacket and extending it toward her.

She takes the package and unwraps it, looking at it with grateful eyes. "This is a noble thing you have done for the kingdom. The wand will help us face the evil that awaits us." She looks from the wand to me again. "Is there something I can do for you in return?"

I don't need to give it too much thought. "As a matter of fact, there is."

"Then please ask."

"In our battle with Hassan, when we were able to retrieve the wand, we lost someone, a friend. His name was Sinbad. Ember wanted me to ask you if you're able to tell us whether his soul is at peace."

There's silence and the Blue Faerie closes her eyes, focusing her gaze downward. Her body dims and brightens, pulsating with light as she channels her energy elsewhere and back. Finally, she opens her eyes again and faces me.

"I'm sad to say he's not at peace, not just yet."

"How can that be? We have his Roc and we were told by the tribal elders that his soul is joined to it."

"And that is correct. Or rather, it *was* correct. But upon your friend's death, the Roc was released. That's why it returned to you. It paid homage to its former soulmate by returning him to the place he belongs. That's why it came back to your camp. It is yours now."

"Mine? Or one of my comrades?"

"The Roc belongs to all of you. Your souls are connected and thus, you are all tied to it. It will do the bidding of each or any of you and continue until the last of you are gone."

"And what of Sinbad? Where does his soul reside if he's not at peace?"

"I'm sorry to say his soul resides in the caves where his life was lost."

"I don't understand."

She nods as if she realizes she needs to explain. "Hassan is wicked. Rather than allowing Sinbad's soul to escape, Hassan trapped it inside the cave in the moments after Sinbad used the wand and died from its enormous power."

"Is there anything we can do to help him?"

"Perhaps," she answers and appears confused by this point as she shakes her head. "It's difficult to say. The caves are a treacherous place even without the djinn, Hassan. Where is he now?"

"I don't know. He disappeared after Sinbad hit him with the wand you now hold in your hands."

The Blue Faerie nods as she glances down at the wand again—truly, it is a source of both incredible beauty and death and destruction. "That is unfortunate, but Hassan shall rear his ugly head again. Of that, you can be certain."

That's when Tinker speaks up. She's a lovely, tiny creature. Even a mortal like me can feel the warmth and kindness flowing through the air when she speaks, no doubt, part of her magic.

"Please tell Ember that I will do whatever I can to bring the peace she desires to Sinbad and to allow them to share a final goodbye."

"Thank you," I reply. "I'll take my leave of you then."

I hurry out of the cottage and back to the Roc, eager to return to Ember.

When I return, I find Ember in her bed chamber, with Aimes and Blake. Of course, they're all in the nude and clearly haven't waited for me to return, but are busily enjoying one another's bodies.

"Is it too much to ask that you bastards might wait for me… ever?" I grumble.

"Oh, stop your complaining," Blake responds as he pulls away from kissing our bride. "We've warmed her up for you."

Her lithe body rocks forward and back on Aimes's hard cock, which is planted firmly inside her from behind.

"Looks like you warmed her up for Aimes," I mutter as I approach them. I simply stand there as I watch Aimes wrap his hand around her long hair, using it like a bridle to pull her head slightly up and back.

He pulls out of her but doesn't release his hold on her hair. Meanwhile, I drop my trousers and approach her, glorying in the view before me. Her buttocks are high and round, full in a way that fills up my palms.

I thrust my already rigid cock deeply inside her and then pull out, motioning for Aimes to return to his position. He doesn't hesitate, but immediately thrusts inside her as I walk around to her face and lean down to kiss her. Then, wanting her to taste herself on me, I hold my cock to her mouth. She eagerly opens her lips and I plunge myself all the way down her throat. She moans, sending vibrations along the length of me, immediately pushing me close to the edge.

Blake seems to be enjoying the show as much as we are participating in it. Ember bobs back and forth between Aimes and myself, happily impaled on both ends by our generous length and girth. She makes enough noise to let anyone within earshot know what pleasure she's getting from her three husbands.

Ember's body begins to quiver, shaking violently as she screams out her ecstasy. The buzzing on my cock takes me even closer to the edge. But she's even closer than I am. She orgasms in waves of bliss, vibrating the head of my cock and then relaxing again.

Aimes releases a long, low growl that seems to rise from his belly and explode outward. He sinks into her one last time and climaxes, his body shaking with the intense power of his release. He lingers only for a moment before pulling free and collapsing on a nearby chaise.

Eager to be inside her again, I pull out of her mouth, giving her a chance to catch her breath while I reposition myself behind her. As soon as I'm in the right spot, I slip myself slowly into her lubricated folds. I know I'm too large for some women. If not for the warmup, courtesy of Aimes, that might be the case with Ember, too. But her walls wrap snugly around my cock, like a tight-fitting glove. She lets out a howl as I inch forward, burying a good ten inches inside her small orifice.

Bored by merely watching the show, Blake assumes his place in front of her, offering his own generous length. She moans and swirls her tongue over the tip of his tool, licking her way down each side, and pumping the length of it with her hands, which look even tinier against his sizable shaft.

I perfect my strokes, seesawing in and out of her as I approach my pleasure. But I keep staving it off so I can bring her even more. I swirl my finger through the slickness that clings to the edges of her clit, stroking it. Her immediate reaction is to buck against me. Moving upward, I rub my wet thumb slowly around the entrance to her ass, loving her responses caused by the combination of mine and Blake's efforts.

"Yes, harder," she gasps between wet mouthfuls of cock. She starts spasming again, her body shuddering with the explosions taking place inside her. Blake slides fully inside her mouth, cutting off her cries of joy with steady strokes. She gurgles on him as he pushes against her throat. Then he pulls out so only the tip of his cock stays inside her lips, allowing her to catch her breath.

Meanwhile, I don't let up with my strokes. I keep fucking her while alternately massaging her clit and anus until she's twitching and moaning on Blake's cock, having multiple orgasms. Her juices drip down my hands and my cock is so close to coming. But I'm not finished yet.

She's so beautiful like this, her skin glistening with sweat as I divide her again and again. I'm mesmerized while watching it and I reach for her long hair, pulling her head backward to give Blake a better angle while I engage her with every bit of pleasure I can offer. I notice how her strands of hair seem to shimmer even in the dimly lit room, and the almost invisible scale pattern under her skin gives off a light glow. It's fascinating and beautiful to watch and I finally surrender. But before I fill her with my seed, I pull out and let it flow onto her back.

I release her hair and drop back to watch her beautiful form while she focuses on Blake's needs.

I once again observe the delicate scale pattern that glows from beneath her skin when she's excited.

Blake finishes in her mouth, letting her lick and suck his cock until he finally releases the fruit of her labors, letting it slide down the back of her throat until he slips free. He leans down and kisses her with the taste of his climax still on her breath.

Much to my surprise, she's unbothered by the mess we've all made of her. Ordinarily, a speck of dust on her frock is enough to alarm her. But here she is now, completely disheveled—beautifully so, I might add—and she doesn't seem the least bit upset. Instead, she calmly settles against the bed with Blake curled around her back and me lying in front of her. I'm completely taken by how incredible she is, the sweat dripping from her glorious breasts and our sticky emissions clinging to her thighs, back and face.

Overcome with unfamiliar emotions, I cup her chin in my hand and kiss her passionately. I'm surprised to find myself getting aroused again so soon. And apparently, I'm not the only one. She pulls me closer and rolls me on my back to straddle me. Taking my cock in her hands, she massages me until I'm rock hard once again. I watch her impale herself on me, riding my cock with wild abandon.

My hips thrust to meet hers as I allow her to take everything she wants from me, watching her breasts bounce up and down as her slim body swallows my girth. She slides all the way upward so the tip of my cock is visible and then drops heavily downward again, yelping a bit when I hit bottom.

I grunt loudly as she settles down on me one last time, her body vibrating against mine. Her eyes are closed and the scaled pattern emerges once more. Then she explodes from her very core. I join her, releasing yet another heavy load, this time inside her perfect pink center. I could die now and be grateful.

As her body slowly stops shuddering from the small aftershocks of orgasms, she pulls free of me. She smiles when she spots my saturated cock as it deflates against my belly. I expect we'll all go to sleep now, knowing that all of us would follow this woman to the ends of the Earth and jump off if she commanded it.

EPILOGUE
SINBAD

I make my way through the pastures that spread across the land for miles behind the castle grounds of Sweetland. The sun beams down brightly overhead. I'm grateful for it after spending so long in the dank, dim corridors of the Caves of Larne. I still have no idea how I came to be here. I only know it's good to be free again.

I feel as though I've walked for days without getting very far. I can see the castle in the distance, but it doesn't seem any closer, no matter how far I travel. I'll arrive there, eventually. Indeed, I must. I have to find the others to learn how the battle ended after I was blasted by the wand.

Lying unconscious for a while, I was plunged into darkness and became a senseless thing. When I awoke, everyone was gone. I knew they wouldn't abandon me, so something must have happened. For weeks, I tried to find a way out without success until suddenly, here I stand. No doubt, I'll have to ask the castle physician to take a look at me. The wand's powers may have triggered some strange humors inside me.

Curiously, I've not seen another soul since I emerged from the caves. That is, until I think I see someone in the distance. I try to quicken my pace to get closer, but it seems as though I'm walking through some sort of thick fog. Only after more time passes does the figure finally come into view. Her raiment indicates that of a shepherdess.

As she comes closer, I can see what a tiny thing she is, not at all what I originally believed her to be. I watch her approach before she looks me up and down.

"Are you lost?" she asks.

"I believe so."

"Where have you come from?"

"The Caves of Larne."

"No one escapes from the caves."

"And yet here I stand before you," I say, spreading my hands. I give my surroundings a doubtful gaze. "Wherever 'here' happens to be."

"Oh, you're currently in the Mallow Fields."

"I see," I reply, looking around with a puzzled expression.

I glance at my hand, which appears to be fading in and out. One minute it's solid, and the next, almost completely invisible, like a faint shadow of itself. There must be potent magic in this land.

"Can you see me?" I ask. "I mean, *all* of me?"

"Yes, mostly," the shepherdess replies. "You fade in and out."

"Is that normal for this place?"

"No, not really."

I hum. "What could be causing it?"

"Oh, I can't say."

"Can't or won't?"

"Either way, it changes nothing."

"While that is true, it might help me understand what's going on."

"What is your name?" she asks.

"Sinbad."

The little one seems surprised. "Sinbad?"

"Yes. Why?"

"Oh, nothing," she answers, punctuating her words with a sigh followed by a perceptibly deep breath before she speaks again. "Mine is Bowie P. Bachette, and you, Sinbad, are coming with me."

"I think not," I reply with a broad grin on my face.

~

To Be Continued in
BOWIE

Now Available!

DOWNLOAD FREE EBOOKS!
It's as easy as:

1. Visit my website (hpmallory.com)

2. Sign up in the popup box or the link on the home page

3. Check your email!

HP MALLORY is a New York Times and
USA Today Bestselling Author!

She lives in Southern California with her son, where she is at
work on her next book.
Be sure to visit her at www.hpmallory.com!